THE
WALL

PAUL KRIEGER

Contents

Dedication

Dedicated to the woman architect who chauffeured the author around East Berlin in 1982 and to the author's wife, who married him on the anniversary of the erecting of the Berlin Wall.

Acknowledgment

Book cover background photograph credit to John Zukowsky and the Library of Congress.

Preface

This story originated from time spent during a graduate scholarship to Berlin, West Berlin, to study social housing being built for the Internationale Bauausstellung exhibition. The exhibition's purpose was to demonstrate how urban development could repair the areas of Berlin impacted by the division of the city from the beginning of the Cold War.

The author's focus was diverted by the presence of the Berlin Wall, a boundary that was both architectural and political, unrelenting in its path surrounding the residents, inhabitants, and captives of West Berlin. West Berliners had already come to terms with the Wall, either respecting or ignoring it. The Wall was like a relative to them, residing quietly but omnipresent, serving as a reminder of the limits on their freedoms and the instruction to 'be back home before midnight' if they ventured into East Berlin. Life went on even though the city and its umbilical cord could be cut off easily from the world, once again.

For the East Berliners, their feelings were more opaque, as they were not encircled by the Wall but rather prevented from traveling to a different world, which, after the Wall's removal, was not necessarily the paradise they had hoped for.

Numerous design competitions were held for rebuilding West Berlin, all of which did not address the Wall as it was assumed that it would eventually fade away sometime in the future. But what could an architect or an urban planner do then at that time to accelerate the reunification of Berlin?

The Berlin Wall came down a few years after the graduate scholarship, in an unexpected and sudden manner, with a fitting farewell party as the citizens of Berlin chipped away at it from both sides.

The split personality is now gone, but the historical mental state remains, fortunately, due to some remnants of the Wall along its previous path encircling West Berlin.

Chapter One

The Lake Michigan water, while rough, glimmered like a continuous carpet of sparkles stretching out from the Chicago shoreline to the isolated water intake crib far from the shore, the source of fresh water flowing through an umbilical-cord tunnel below the sand bed to feed the city. The water intake crib, this artificial island of habitable water engineering, was an outpost in the lake, but for Titus, it was a refuge to think about his past, forget the present, and wonder about the future. Architecture was his life but no more, not right now.

Titus had earlier negotiated a workspace in the crib through his contacts in the city engineering department. As a studio retreat, and even though the interior of the crib was utilitarian with a touch of desolation, he used the circular bare walls of the intake crib house as display space, working through his sketches, his initial "love letters" to his projects. The isolation of the water intake crib reinforced his concentration on his designs, an escape into his ideas being delivered by his hand and ink pen. The sketching on paper now relieved him of intrusive thoughts of the near past, and the consistent sound of the water washing up against the walls of the crib provided the background for his sketching. His hand was now stopped by the click and whir of the fax machine in the crib-house office.

Titus's concentration was now broken, and he stood and walked around the crib house, looking at the sketches on the walls. He was again interrupted by the final beeps of the fax machine, finishing its message. He looked at the fax machine and noted a familiar header on the sheet of paper sticking out. TITUS DARE ARCHITECTS – Chicago * London * Berlin.

He pulled the paper out of the fax machine, looked at it, and then discarded it into the pile of similar faxes, but something caught his eye. This faxed page had the word URGENT written right below the header. He picked it back up with both hands, which tensed as he read it. He moved to the sketches on the wall, pulled a sketch off, carried it over to the desk, and laid the fax and sketch on the table. He focused on the sketch of a building that resembled a gateway. He ran his finger over the sketch and looked at the fax once more.

The fax read:

August 13, 1985

Titus,

Just received a fax from Berlin. They need you in Berlin on the Tor Project. Call me at the office.

David

The phone rang as Titus read the fax, and he picked up the phone. David, the office manager of Titus Dare Architects, spoke softly but firmly, "Titus, I'm glad I finally reached you. It would help if you answered the phone while you were out there."

After a pause that Titus did not fill, David continued, "The call came in about a week ago, and I did not know how you wanted to respond. I understand how you needed some time alone after what happened, but . . ."

Titus replied, "I was sure this was dead, like a number of things in my life."

"No, I was surprised too," David said. "Apparently, they have been working on it pretty much the way you designed it, with some modifications. I'm not sure what that means, but they want you to be at the foundation stone setting next week, which is always the big deal in Germany."

David continued, "Titus, it would be good for you to get out of your exile and get active. The office is basically on hold, and it would be great to be designing something again with some staff around here. Everybody wants to come back to work." He was looking around at the empty office, which was once an active hub for creativity with all the feel of a high-design interior and now sporting a layer of dust and silence.

"Why do they need me if they have been working on it without me?" Titus replied.

"In my opinion, you have to put all that behind you. The people on the project in Berlin have been patient, given the circumstances, but the projects will continue when they are this far along . . . with or without us. Better with us, in my opinion, and better for you. Time for you to get back to you."

Titus thought for a moment. "I'm not sure that's such a good idea necessarily."

"No, there's no doubt it was an unpleasant scene for you, but for better or worse, excuse me for speaking very personally, you have to put that behind you," David said. "And you need to work through it, no matter how it made you look or feel. The work will get this behind you."

Titus paused again, then said, "I trust your take on this. Perhaps Berlin would be a good distraction. A retreat from a retreat and another little island connected by a thread."

"Great. Trust me, it will be for the best. You never made it to Berlin during the design competition anyway. So, a trip to Berlin may be enough to make even your current state of mind look normal. It was . . . is a historic opportunity to work right on the Berlin Wall, and our design was picked over a healthy field of architects, from all over the world. And not to mention the significance of an office building for future diplomatic relationships between the two German countries. A symbolic tour de force, if I do say so myself."

"Not sure what normal feels like, but thanks for the insight."

"That was a compliment, if you couldn't tell." David's tone was apologetic. "You need to lighten up and start living, start designing again."

"Are you coming on the visit?" asked Titus.

"The invite is for you only. This will be good for you. And I'll have one of our German contacts meet you at the airport in Frankfurt. Try to focus on getting back into design mode."

Hanging up the phone, Titus continued to look at his drawings on the desk and pulled a large drawing across the top. It was the rendering for the project in Berlin. The drawing showed the Berlin Wall interrupted by an office building with a gateway in the center through the wall. The project name on the drawing was Berlin Tor—ein Tor, as the Germans called it.

David hung up, looked at the phone for a moment, and then looked to the side, focusing his attention on someone else in the office.

A heavily accented voice responded to David's gaze. "Na, very good, Mr. Fielding. Your cooperation on this is most appreciated. Here is a reward for your help with the call to persuasion."

David responded sharply, "Keep your envelope. He needs to

do this with or without your visit here or any bonus for me. I still work for him."

The voice responded, "Macht nichts. It is very important that he is pushed in the right direction."

"I can only get him there. He is not your typical person. He works for himself first and then for his clients. Not a compromising sort," David retorted.

"Then he will have a very interesting time in Berlin. Goodbye, Mr. Fielding. Until we see each other again." The man left the office without another word.

David looked around the deserted office again, the drafting tables and turned-off lights, shook his head and started sketching on the pad of paper in front of him.

Chapter Two

Titus arrived at the airport in Chicago and made his way through the check-in process. He boarded the airplane and settled into his seat. The aluminum cocoon of the airplane would take him to his project and perhaps undo some of the recent past. As the airplane took off, his mind slipped into sleep with a dream of the past, of a familiar voice and the female lips behind them. From the lips came, "But I have planned our private birthday party, just you and me for once. I baked a birthday cake just for you and planned a night out with a hotel room downtown. Remember, we were going to start working on a family."

Titus's voice returned in response, "They moved up the topping-out ceremony to today because of the schedule. I can't miss this. One night won't make a difference whether we . . . this is very important."

The female voice urged, "So are we. I have stayed with you through all this, and now it's time for you to stay with me. Time for those creative juices to be focused on me and our future, instead of your buildings."

Titus's voice responded equally in determination, "I will be home as soon as I can after the ceremony."

The female voice said, "You need to make some

compromises . . . no, not compromises, but decisions about me and not yourself. There is this wall of your work that you have put up, where it doesn't allow you to let anyone in or to let you out."

Titus's voice became detached, "I will be home as soon as I can, I promise."

The female voice responded, "Don't bother. I give up . . . I will meet you at your building. I can see where I stand in all this."

Titus responded sharply, "You do not have to do that."

A final resolve came from the female voice but without hope, "I have competed for your attention with your work for too long. You choose—come home as we planned, or the cake is going to come to you," ending with a click of a phone.

Titus's dream image of the female voice dissolved into a vision of a view over the city from a building's top floor, filled with construction workers mixed with a group of dignitaries surrounding Titus. Titus smiled in his dream at the scene of the topping-out ceremony, one of his favorite moments as an architect. As he conversed with the workers and dignitaries, he looked around the construction area on the floor to notice the caged construction elevator arriving. As the elevator door opened, a glow appeared in front of his wife exiting the elevator—the glow coming from a birthday cake in her hands. His first thought was that she should be wearing a hard hat, but the look in her eyes made him focus on her face, which had a blank but determined look. She walked toward the center of the crowd of construction workers, directly at Titus. Someone in the crowd started singing 'Happy Birthday,' and the rest of the crowd joined in.

Titus opened his arms to greet her, but she walked right up to him, handed him the cake, and continued past him, striding across the building floor and towards the edge of the building. Titus began walking after her, cake in hand and then started running as she neared the edge. Dropping the cake, he reached for her scarf, but off the edge she stepped through the protective edge barrier, which was the only thing that stopped Titus from following her off the edge. As he looked below, she had fallen into the safety netting on the floor below. As he looked down at her, she looked up at him with her same blank stare.

Coming out of the vision of his wife's birthday greeting surprise, his dream was interrupted by a stewardess asking him if he was alright and an announcement about the plane's landing.

Departing the plane and moving through customs, Titus exited the airport and turned his eyes upward to the sound of a jet's engine overhead.

Looking around, Titus was brought fully back to his current presence, suitcase and briefcase in hand, standing at the arrivals curb of Frankfurt Airport. A man across the drive lane waved to him.

Titus thought that he must be his contact, based on the man's European architect appearance, wearing all black clothes and metallic round glasses. Titus began to step off the curb in the man's direction, and a car—or what appeared to be a car that sounded like a go-kart and belched blue smoke—almost ran Titus over, hitting his bag in the process. The man ran across the drive lane and reached Titus to steady him, pulling him back onto the curb. Titus looked at his bag for damage, then at the plume of smoke disappearing into the distance, and then to the man.

Titus, still shaken a bit, asked, "What was that thing?" and then added, "Thanks, er, danke. That looked like a cartoon car with its tailpipe on fire."

"Vorsicht, you must be careful there. Titus, Titus Dare, is that correct?" asked the man.

"Yes, that is me."

"Good to meet you. I am Klaus Kohl, one of the coordinating architects for your project in Berlin."

"Pleased to meet you as well," Titus said. "So, what was that vehicle that nearly ended my visit?"

"That was a Trabant from East Germany, sort of a lawnmower that holds people. Ossies are mostly inside, people within East Germany, that is, but every once and awhile, they escape to the West and beyond."

"The car or the people in it?" replied Titus.

"Sometimes just the car. The peoples' pride of the East German auto industry—perhaps we should call it a Volkswagen from the East, courtesy of our Genossen."

"It seems out of place compared to the other cars around here," said Titus, gesturing toward other cars moving through the airport.

Klaus replied, "A divided country creates many refugees, both human and machines. Your Mr. Fielding from your office asked me to ensure a safe journey for you from Frankfurt to Berlin."

"Safe? Well, you are off to a good start, for my sake."

"Smooth, is what I mean to say," Klaus added with a smile. "How was your flight?"

"Uneventful until I stepped off the curb here," Titus said and then thought to himself, *five thousand miles by plane over an ocean, and I almost get hit by a refugee egg-beater.* "By the way, are those more dangerous to ride in or get hit by? Looks like a clown car."

"Sometimes both," Klaus Kohl replied. "I have your train tickets here to Berlin . . . West Berlin, that is. It leaves in the evening, so I will show you around Frankfurt until then. I am not quite sure why they did not fly you straight into Berlin. Something about letting you experience the ride through East Germany to West Berlin."

"Train is just fine," replied Titus. "Better to see the country. Better than driving in a Trabant or whatever they are called. I presume there are more of those things in Berlin. So, what is the schedule for me?"

Klaus pulled a file sleeve from his briefcase and looked at the itinerary. "You arrive into West Berlin in the morning. Here is the train ticket, one way. It is an overnight train with a shared compartment, First-Class. They have also included the booking for your hotel. You have that day to sleep, relax, or go see Berlin if you like. Viel zu sehen. A lot to see in Berlin. And then you are to go to the site the next morning to discuss the project."

Titus asked, "Can you recommend anything to see there? I was doing so many projects during the time of the design competition that I am embarrassed to say I never toured Berlin. Sad to admit. Not my preference on how to give my best effort to a project, not visiting the site first."

"There are many grand buildings and a lot of ruins . . . and a lot of ghosts from our history in Berlin, in particular. Many tourists go to see the Wall that divides the city, and your project.

Strange interest in seeing the Wall, such a source of such misery and division. Divided cities can create some Angst . . . anxiety," Klaus said.

"Considering the nature of my project, that would probably be a good idea to see, the Wall and the site, all things considered," Titus said.

"It is, despite the tragedy of it, just a wall, a basic element of architecture, like a door. It surrounds Berlin, always there, but is ignored by those who live there on both sides. The Berlin Wall is both hard to find and easy to miss in a city split in two, not by choice but by history," Klaus explained. "You realize, of course, West Berlin is an island connected only by the Autobahn, how you say, highway and a rail line, and an uneasy arrangement with the Soviets. You will be traveling through a bit of a prison to reach a circle of freedom in Berlin."

"Must be confusing sometimes," Titus said.

Klaus countered, "Berlin and the Wall are like women—easy to misunderstand and quite strange when you do understand them."

"Sounds accurate to me," Titus said, thinking, *And in line with my relationship with my wife. The Wall and I should get along just fine.*

Klaus motioned toward his car, and they walked to it, with

Klaus putting the luggage in the trunk. Titus opened the passenger-side door and looked around anxiously as a car approached another Trabant, driving behind him in the parking lot.

Klaus smiled. "You have to watch out for those."

"Yes, so you've said."

They drove from the airport through the center of Frankfurt for the promised sightseeing tour.

As they drove, Titus said, "I am still in the dark a little as to why I am here. I know we won the competition for the design, we did the drawings, then my wife . . ." pausing briefly before continuing, "then the project was on its own for a while, and then I suddenly get invited to the cornerstone setting."

"Na, there have been a few difficulties with the project," Klaus started, "that need the designer's, your attention. The Bauherr, the builder, how you say, developer, especially wanted your input, my understanding."

"Well, that's a surprise," Titus said, "as I never did get to meet him, them; it was two brothers, I think I remember, or at least that was the only information we could get. Seemed like nobody really knew who they were, where they came from or how they negotiated the deal. Everything was on a need-to-know basis during the competition. Not used to such secrecy in a building design competition where one is invited to participate."

"Berlin, or the two Berlins," Klaus said, "have a lot of secrets, but the good thing for you is that the cornerstone will be set, and you are invited. Very important ceremony here in Germany and an honor to participate, to strike the cornerstone with the hammer."

The tour continued as they drove, with Titus asking about this or that building and Klaus providing details.

"I think we will stop for a coffee. I know just the place," Klaus offered after an hour of touring.

They pulled up outside of a heavily ornamented Classical-style building from an earlier period in time and said, "There is a café inside the greenhouse, very nice." They entered the ornate stone building that fronted a large, glazed-iron structure from the nineteenth century. They were seated at a table where one could see the cupola of the greenhouse over a statue of a man and woman. The statue, based on Titus's guess, was a representation of Adam and Eve. While waiting for the coffee to arrive, Titus looked up and was intrigued at the birds flying in and out of the cupola vent.

"Interesting that they can fly in and out and know the difference between the outside and the protection of the inside. Like a bubble of security," mused Titus.

Klaus replied, "Like West Berlin, an outpost of safety from

a hostile surrounding. However, once you get to Berlin, you will wonder if the wall is to keep someone out or someone in."

Titus pointed at the statue. "I guess Adam and Eve are inside the planted paradise of Berlin this time."

After the café break, they drove some more and finally pulled the car to the street curb in front of the Frankfurt Hauptbahnhof, the train station. Titus stepped out of the car and repeated his look both ways for a possible hit-and-run attempt. Klaus helped him retrieve his luggage from the car trunk, noted Titus's concern, and said, "I see you have learned to watch out for your four-wheeled friend."

Klaus then handed Titus an envelope. "Here is your ticket. It is a First-Class compartment ticket, and there is the compartment number. Look for the train departing at 20:13 to Berlin, Bahnhof Zoo. That is thirteen minutes past eight o'clock."

Titus took the envelope and looked it over.

Klaus checked his watch. "You must hurry."

Titus shook hands with Klaus and turned toward the train station entrance. Over his shoulder, he heard, "Gute Reise."

Titus turned and asked, "How's that?"

Klaus responded, "Have a good trip and a safe journey. It is an interesting journey, going from one side to the other."

Titus waved back and entered the train-track hall. He looked up at the departure board and noted the destination:

Berlin—Bahnhof Zoo—Gleis 13

He headed out onto the platform, watching passengers loading. Titus showed his ticket to an attendant at one of the train entry doors, who waved him forward, saying, "Erste Klasse, weiter entlang." Based on Titus's puzzled look, the attendant clarified, "First-Class, further down." Titus continued farther along the platform until he saw a number 1 on the train car and climbed aboard.

Inside the train-car passageway, Titus walked slowly along where the entrances to the compartments were. Looking at the train ticket, he noted the number of the compartment and continued on his way to his train compartment. He asked a train porter in the corridor for assistance, and he directed Titus to his compartment. Titus slid the compartment door open and placed his suitcase on the luggage rack. As he turned to his seat, there sat a large man who sized him up by dropping his eyeglasses for a moment. Titus returned the gaze and noticed the man was well dressed but in an out-of-fashion way. He was dressed in a plaid suit that made him look older than he was, and the suit was tight on his body. His face reflected confidence but earned at the price of some stress over time.

"Guten Abend," said the man.

Titus replied, "Hello. I'm afraid I do not speak German."

"That is okay. I do not speak English," the man said with a large smile and a distinct German accent.

"Where are you heading?" asked Titus after a pause.

The man said, "This train only goes to one place."

"Heading to Berlin for business?"

"You could say that. And you?"

"I have a building project there," Titus said, pausing in consideration of how much personal information to give in this situation. "I'm an architect. It is right at the Berlin Wall, actually."

"Architects interest me. They have a vision of the future, and Berlin's future has to have vision," offered the man.

"Why is that?" Titus prompted, thinking the conversation would make the overnight train seem a shorter ride.

"Theirs is the gift of vision and opportunity. Berlin is unique in its opportunity. I am, on the other hand, just a simple businessman."

"Do you own any buildings?"

"You could say that," the man said. "I own some buildings, some people, some dreams." He turned and stared out the train compartment window.

Titus shifted in his seat based on the response and took a

harder look at the man, who now turned and looked back at him. It was an awkward pause while they looked at each other until the train jerked and disrupted their connected stare. The train pulled from the station, and Titus settled back in his seat.

Trying to break the silence, Titus asked, "Will there be more people in the compartment?"

"Perhaps between here and Helmstedt – Marienborn, die Grenze, the border crossing, as you would call it. . . from there to Berlin, no one gets on, and no one gets off. At least not without a good or a bad reason," replied the man with a knowing smile.

"What do you mean?"

"This train travels from Frankfurt to the Grenze, the border, and then through East Germany and back into West Berlin. Then back into East Berlin."

"I forgot about that. My knowledge of geography and sense of politics is probably a little naive. It is coming back to me, though. Berlin is an island, except not surrounded by a sunny beach," Titus said with an affirmative shake of his head.

"You mean West Berlin," corrected the man.

Titus accepted the comment with a nod, closed his eyes, and dozed off. His mind, in a dream, went back to the past of what he had just left and forward to a fuzzy image of where he was going.

His drifting mind was interrupted by the sound of the train stopping with a jerk. He looked at his watch and noted, to his surprise, that he had been asleep for about four hours, but then he recognized the effect of his jet lag.

"Where are we? Why are we stopping?" Titus asked, more as an open question, ". . . and why is it so bloody cold now?"

The man said, "We are at die Grenze, the border, and they are changing over to the East German locomotives. Enough power to pull the train but not enough to keep the people warm, on trains, and . . . in apartments." Titus sensed the man was amused by the answer in both a dismissive and sympathetic manner.

Titus directed his attention to the sounds of voices, compartment doors opening and closing, and footsteps out in the train passageway, and he started looking out in the passageway from his seat. As the noises came closer and more serious in tone, Titus settled back in his seat. There was a pause in the noise, and then their compartment door opened. A guard with a holstered handgun came in. Titus studied his uniform, similar to the uniforms he had seen in Frankfurt, but there was a distinct darkness in the guard's attitude with the now dimmer lights in the compartment. The dimness was accompanied by a smell of burned coal that came with the compartment door open, a noticeable haze outside the window, and a certain disconnect between the secure bubble of his train compartment and the guard's presence now.

"Pass, bitte," said the guard.

"Beg your pardon?" replied Titus, surprised but gradually recognizing the guard as West German.

His compartment companion said, "He would like to see your passport."

Despite the clarity of the request and a better understanding of the situation, Titus still fumbled for his passport and finally handed it to the guard, who stared at the other man and then back at Titus. The guard flipped through the pages of the passport and looked at Titus several times while examining it. Titus's anxiousness increased, more based on the sheer reality of the situation than thinking that something was wrong with his passport.

The guard asked in a stiff voice, "Wohin?"

Titus stared at him blankly and was cautious about initiating any misunderstanding.

The guard looked impatient but then softened. "Where are you traveling to?"

Titus replied, "To Berlin. I thought this train does not go anywhere else?"

The guard focused his eyes on Titus. "East or West?" he asked with a slight grin.

Titus looked around the train compartment, thinking about the right answer. "West . . . I hope."

The guard responded, "Danke," but returned to a certain stiffness. He turned to the other man in the compartment. "Pass, bitte," he said, continuing with an official tone and focusing on the man.

The other man returned the guard's stare in equal measure and handed the guard his passport with an air of superiority. The guard held his gaze and pressed his other hand on his radio on his shoulder, and he then flipped through some pages in the passport. He seemed to react with his surprise, given his raised eyebrow, at whatever he had just seen.

Titus watched the interaction with interest. He noticed the guard came to a more focused, enquiring, perhaps deferential stance. Titus watched as the guard handed back the passport and looked at the other man for some understanding of the guard's behavior. The man gave the guard a dismissive look, reflected in the way he took his passport back from the guard.

This seems odd, thought Titus, and he looked at the man again for some understanding of the interaction.

As the guard backed away through the compartment door, he spoke softly to the man, "Gute Reise," and then turned to Titus with a similar apologetic tone, "Good luck in Berlin. Viel Glueck."

Titus looked first at the guard in surprise and then at the man curiously as the door closed. "What did he say?" Titus asked.

The man looked at Titus, paused, then said, "He wished you good luck, much luck. But really, he wanted to practice his English."

"Odd to wish me good luck," Titus said.

"Better than to say goodbye, do you not think?" quipped the man in response.

"Friendly, aren't they, the guards, huh?" commented Titus.

"Sometimes. It is his job," the man said with a wry smile.

"I noticed he seemed to recognize you, or your passport?"

"Na ja, I am on this train quite often with business on both sides. Sometimes, there is a new guard to make my acquaintance."

"Both sides?" asked Titus.

"Both sides of the Wall, of Berlin, of Germany."

Titus nodded and looked out the window as a hissing sound occurred outside and under the train. "Just like my building project, straddling the Wall. Still odd that the guard wished me good luck."

"Maybe a wish of good luck is somehow appropriate. Or maybe he knows something about Berlin you do not," was the man's reply with a larger and somewhat knowing smile.

Titus stood up and looked out the train window for the

source of the hissing sound. He expected the train to start moving, but no movement yet.

"Is that the Wall with the barbed wire on top?" Titus asked, looking back at the man.

"Ja, die Mauer," was the response.

"Die Mauer?" asked Titus, looking up and down the train tracks in both directions.

"Yes, it is German for the word 'wall.' It is a feminine noun in German," the man said.

In the haze of the bright lights around the Wall, Titus could see the whiteness of the Wall and various guard watchtowers overlooking the Wall. "So, is that what it, she, looks like all the way? Is this where it starts?"

"It is the beginning of it or the end, depending on which side you are on. Remember, it is a circle. You are entering the first circle, then to a second circle, ein bisschen Inferno-like, except not Limbo nor Lust, that is for sure."

Titus was focused on one element that he could see, staring now intently at a crude glass shelter on an old train platform on the side of the tracks. He looked back into the compartment. "But it just runs right through the shelter there, like it had a mind of its own. In architecture, we would call that an awkward detail," remarked Titus with a smile.

"Doch, die Mauer . . . the Wall does have its own path, making its own way, like a headstrong woman—though not through men, but through politics," the man philosophized. "She may be too direct and perhaps clumsy in execution, but effective."

Titus thought about the comparison. "Yes, I can see the comparison. For an architect and walls being one of our main tools, 'she,' as you would say, is certainly blunt as a division, not much refinement, as far as I can see from here. God is in the details is the common architect's saying. The Wall might need some help."

The man shook his head slightly. "More likely der Teufel, the devil is in the details. Na ja, it was put up quite quickly. It was a necessary thing to keep everyone in the correct place. It keeps Cain and Abel apart. And Cain is very jealous of Abel."

"I assume you mean Cain is East Berlin," Titus said.

A grin from the man. "Sometimes. Depends on where you are and where you want to be."

Titus reached into his jacket, pulled out his small camera, and tried to get an angled shot out of the train window he opened.

"That is not advisable," the man said in a polite but firm tone. "This is a very sensitive area, of the border."

Titus took a quick photograph and slipped the camera back into his jacket pocket. He turned back to the train compartment window.

The train started to move with a jolt, and Titus grabbed the edge of the window for support, swinging back into his seat. The reality of the division, the Wall, physical and political, was beginning to sink in for Titus. It was not a garden wall but one with barbed wire, guards, guns, and all the prison-like associations. The view from the train window now seemed just like a fuzzy glow of lights moving through the mist into the East. His sense of adventure, like starting a new project or traveling to a new city, was weakening slightly into apprehension.

The man perceived Titus's beginning unease. "It is a long journey into the night. You should get some sleep, but they will come again." Then the man clarified, "The guards."

Titus settled into his seat, wondering about more guards, then folded his arms against the cold and wrapped his scarf around his neck. The train lurched again and continued to move forward.

Titus tried to sink into his thoughts and any peace he could find there, traveling back in his mind to the inner satisfaction he found in design—understanding a problem and finding a solution. Another jolt of the train brought Titus back. But there was a new sensation, not a visual one but nasal. "What is that smell?"

"That is the warmth of East Germany. Coal bricks used for oven heating here," the man said casually.

Titus stood and stretched his legs, looking out the window. He observed, "A lot of pollution, isn't it? The lights all have halos, like good saints."

"Yes, they do. The East Germans have sacrificed much for their paradise," affirmed the man. "That smell is how you can tell an East German, sometimes."

Titus peered deeper into the haze. "Why are all the television antennae pointed to the West, like someone combed them in one direction?"

"Better reception to the West and sometimes better TV programs over there. A glimpse into the decadent West to remind themselves how lucky they are in the East."

"I am intrigued to meet a real East German . . . what their life is really like. Trapped behind a wall and isolated . . ." He stopped there, recalling his words and watching the man, then thought better of continuing.

"It is not seen that way. West Berlin is trapped inside the Wall. You will see. Sometimes inside is out, and outside is in. As I said, the Wall was built to keep the West out in one sense for some. You will see."

Titus thought about it and said to himself, "I guess I will. I myself have been outside of things for a while."

He settled back into his seat and shut his eyes. In his mind, he looked into the halo of light on a lamppost, which became a hazy image of a woman's face, his wife's face, the curves, the shadows, the lines, and the eyes. That face dissolved as the train halted again. Titus could hear the sound of dogs barking. He could see guards with flashlights and long-stem mirrors searching under the train cars, following the dogs.

"What are they looking for?"

"People," the man said.

Surprised but now not surprised by his current experience, Titus responded, "People sneaking into East Germany?"

"Sometimes," replied the man without hesitation.

"Why would anyone do that?"

"The Wall also keeps out enemies of the state. Spies, I think you call them."

Their conversation was interrupted as the compartment door opened with a loud thud. A new face, a female one, entered his vision. It was a female guard at the door, an unfriendly-looking one, in a different uniform, less tailored, browner with a distinct smell of smoke, of coal and cigarettes. Behind her stood a male version of her with a similar demeanor.

"Pass, bitte!" came the voice with a harsh tone of authority.

Startled, Titus worked his hands over his pockets to find his passport. Finding it, he offered it to the guard over her machine gun that was pointing right at his face. The guard surveyed him from his eyes down to his shoes. Titus moved his head away from the barrel of the gun and shifted in his seat. He was tempted to try to move the gun away with his finger, as if he were in a movie—a dash of secret-agent humor. He was relieved as the guard removed her hand from the gun grip and flipped through pages on the flip-down tablet she had hanging from her neck.

She looked at the pages in the passport and then turned to Titus. "What is your business in Berlin?"

"I am an architect, with a building in Berlin, West Berlin, that is . . . well, I guess it is in East Berlin as well."

"Then you must pay attention to which train station to get off at. Bahnhof Zoo, nicht weiter. Viel Glueck damit."

The guard turned to the man in the train compartment. "Pass, bitte." She gave the man a dutiful look after briefly looking at his passport with a nod of her head and a slight click of her heels, or at least that was Titus's impression. Based on the guard's deference, Titus peered at the man's passport as the guard handed it back to the man. He now noticed it was a different color than his, but he could not see any markings on the passport.

After the guard pulled the door shut upon leaving, Titus

turned back to the man, "I assume 'viel Glueck' means good luck, like the other guard? Another thoughtful wish." Pausing, "This guard seemed to recognize you, sort of like the other guard."

The man replied coolly, "Wie gesagt, I travel here quite often. Also, I am German. She recognizes a brother."

Titus took that in. "Why the second look at my passport? The second guard?"

"The second one, she was guarding from spies entering East Germany; the first one, he was guarding West Berlin from undesirables," the man explained.

Titus pondered the logistics of this.

The man continued, "Na ja, as I said, it is two circles here. The first group of guards were from the West, watching for leaving West Germany and entering West Berlin. The second group were from the East, for entering East Germany and East Berlin."

Titus stood up and looked out the window as the train began to move again.

"It will be a while now, not much to see through the night. You have a very busy time ahead of you, I feel," the man said, closing his eyes.

Titus looked out the train window for a time and then returned to his seat and closed his eyes as well, pulling his scarf and coat around him. He listened to the train moving. The clack of the wheels on the tracks had a rhythm, like a clock ticking on a nightstand. It was reassuring in its consistency, but as Titus thought about it, just as the landscape outside had changed and the level of heat in the train compartment had changed, this sound was new.

Titus opened his eyes with this thought and noticed the man was watching him.

The man asked, "Etwas? Can you not sleep?"

"The train sounds different. It was very quiet before, but now there is a clicking sound, regular in timing."

"You are very perceptive, a true architect. All senses working and always aware. That is the difference in the rails. They are, how you say, welded in West Germany, but only bolted together here in the East."

"That explains it. This is like passing through a portal, crossing over into a different existence."

"You will find there are other differences. You should keep your senses open," said the man, touching his own nose very gently on the side.

The train continued into the night, into the darkness, and into Titus's future. He drifted into a light sleep, feeling like he was breathing carbon monoxide from outside the train.

Titus's light sleep was interrupted by a brighter glow of lights outside the train windows. He undid his coat and moved to the window, looking around.

"It looks very different here. Are we in West Berlin?"

"Same people, same buildings, different cars. Just a line between them and where they were when the Wall went up," replied the man.

Titus remained by the window as the houses and buildings became more frequent. At first, there were single houses and some villas, then village centers and bridges, and finally, the urban texture of Berlin began. He looked more intently at the apartments and office buildings, and the lights became stronger with colors and signs of a metropolis. The elevated route of the train into the city allowed Titus to peer down on the people—no different than in Chicago. He sensed the excitement of a new place, a new city, a new chance to design and build.

As the train slowed, he leaned closer to the window, looking in the direction the train was headed. He saw a glazed arch structure. "What's this station?" he asked over his shoulder.

"Bahnhof Zoo as in *Zoologischer Garten*. Same as your animal zoos, the zoo is next to the train station."

"This is the main station? It's just a train shed," Titus said, looking for the man's concurrence.

"It is the main train station for West Berlin. That is where you are going, richtig? The real main station is in East Berlin, behind the Wall, in the center of Berlin. It is only a short stop here, so you should go."

"Are you sure that I get off here? Don't they warn you more than that?" asked Titus with some anxiety building. He started to frantically pull his luggage down from the rack and looked at the man still sitting. "Aren't you getting off?"

"No, I have business in the East."

Titus did not know what to make of that possibility, and he thought, *So he is from East Germany?* With a nod of his head, he said, "Well, thanks for the company, and information."

"Auf Wiedersehen," the man said. "That means 'until we see each other again.'"

"Auf Veedersehen," returned Titus, not quite sure about the pronunciation. "Well, goodbye. I mean, until next time."

THE WALL

Chapter Three

Titus exited the train compartment and walked down the passageway of the train car, looking out of the windows at a deserted train platform. Once on the platform, he looked back toward the compartment he had come from as the train slowly started to pull out. The man in the compartment provided a half wave in the glow coming from the window.

A few other passengers got off the train, and Titus followed them down a dimly lit staircase to the street with his luggage. The shop area inside the train station offered a number of punk rockers, lost-looking souls, and other typical train-station inhabitants, more like refugees really, he thought. He noticed that the posters and display vitrines had been sprayed with words and anarchist symbols. The food shops offered an aroma to match the visuals of a complete atmosphere of survival from and escape into urban decay.

Exiting the train station at street level, he looked at the bright lights of stores and signs—tourist shops, 'schnell imbiss,' and peep-show shops, and patches of darkness in doorways where people stood. *So this is West Berlin, I think, I hope*, he thought.

Titus walked along the street, trying to see a street sign on the main street, curious about where he was for future reference. *Kurfuerstendamm*, he read and then tried to pronounce it and remember it. He looked down the street and discerned that the multitude of yellow Mercedes Benz sedans were taxicabs. Stepping out of the shadows to a streetlight, he raised his hand to hail a cab. A noisy car swerved from its lane and almost hit him as he started into the street. As it kept going past him, sputtering out a plume of smoke, he recognized it as the same type of car that almost ran him over at Frankfurt airport. He searched his memory—*ah, a Trabant.* He gave it a crusty look, returned his gaze to the street, and raised his hand again. A late-model, pale-yellow taxicab pulled up to him.

"This is West Berlin, correct?" he asked through the driver's window.

"Ja, glaub schon," replied the taxi driver, appearing amused but serious at the same time. The driver looked at Titus, sizing him up, and said, "I believe so," and then looked beyond Titus as if the taxi driver did not know where he was.

Titus looked around again, following where the taxi driver was looking. "I just arrived and got off the train, so I hope I got off at the right place."

No validating response came from the driver, who just looked back at Titus, so Titus ventured, "Do you speak English?"

"Vielleicht, do you speak German?"

"West Berlin, here? It looks like it," said Titus aloud, and then quietly to himself, "and it does not smell."

"It stinks here sometimes too. You are in the West. Wohin?" asked the driver.

"Pardon?"

"Where to?"

"Oh. I need to go to my hotel in Berlin. Hotel Zwielicht."

"There are two Berlins. May be one in East Berlin. Which one?" asked the taxi driver.

"West Berlin," confirmed Titus.

"Na, gut," said the taxi driver, who then opened his door and nodded Titus toward the rear door. The driver then put Titus's luggage in the car trunk.

As they drove off, Titus asked, "Which direction is East Berlin, by the way?"

"East of here," came the answer in the rearview mirror, while Titus was still estimating the seriousness or humor of the driver.

"Which way is east? That way?" Titus pointed in a direction.

"Da und dort. Here and there," said the driver, and he vaguely pointed in one direction and then another with a now-obvious smile on his face.

"You sure you are a taxi driver?" Titus responded, accepting the challenge in wits.

"I am not lost, am I?" countered the driver.

"I am curious. Can you even drive your taxi, into the East?" asked Titus.

"No. Can you?" quipped the driver, clearly entertained by the back-and-forth exchange.

"Good point, so we will just focus on getting me to the hotel," Titus said, deciding to steer the talk and taxicab back to his purpose.

The taxi continued through the bright streets and into the night. Titus sized up what he saw compared to what he had seen in other cities. The same bright lights and obvious luxury stores with shoppers, and then some more private-looking club storefronts with stray women in high heels and fishnets.

After a few turns, the taxi pulled up to a hotel with a sign that read: **HOTEL ZWIELICHT.**

Titus climbed out of the taxicab as the driver walked to the trunk. Titus realized he had not looked at the taxi meter before exiting, pulled out his wallet, and realized he had only U.S. dollars. *This will be interesting*, he thought, as he did not know the exchange rate. He pulled a range of dollar denominations and spread them out like a deck of cards.

"How much for the ride?" asked Titus.

The driver looked at the fan of money bills, then at Titus. He pulled out a selected number of dollar bills, looked at Titus again, and put one of the notes back in Titus's hand.

"I think you will need that," the driver said as he climbed back into the taxicab and looked out the car window. "Danke, thank you. Enjoy Berlin! Oh, best not to pay that way in East Berlin."

Titus watched the taxicab drive off into the darkness wondering whether he had overpaid for the ride and whether it really mattered. He would have to pay attention to the exchange rate and thought, *Is there a separate exchange rate for West Germany and East Germany?*

He entered the hotel's main door and walked up to the reception counter with his luggage. It was a hotel designed in the 1960s, partially luxury finishes in a semi-Brutalist style shell. He stood at the check-in counter, waiting for the female receptionist to look up.

"Bitte?" she asked.

"Titus Dare, I have a reservation."

"Achh, Herr Dare, we have been expecting you. How was your trip to West Berlin?"

"Interesting. Good. The taxi driver was very interesting."

"Ja, they have to be. May I see your passport?"

Titus pulled out his passport and added, "Just glad to be

where I am supposed to be.”

“Titus Dare, that is an interesting name. D-A-R-E. It means to take a chance, no?” she asked.

“Yes, that is right. Not always true for me, but I think Berlin will be a challenge.”

“Just a few questions for the registration. Are you married?” she asked.

“No, not really. I mean, no,” sputtered Titus.

“Occupation?” she followed.

“Architect.”

“Then you should have no trouble finding something interesting here,” said the receptionist with a smile. “Lots of history, many buildings, maybe some haunted by history.”

“I don’t think that will be a problem. The Wall already seems interesting enough,” he said, and he noticed a shadow coming over the receptionist’s smile.

“Please sign here,” she said a little more curtly. “And here is your key, Room 813.”

Titus gave a polite smile back to redeem what seemed to be a sensitive topic and thought to himself, *Have to watch this Wall thing, I suppose.* He walked to the hotel elevator, entered, and pushed the number 813 button, hoping that the number thirteen was not a sign of things to come.

Once on his floor, Titus walked down the somewhat dimly lit corridor, looking for his room number. Finding it, he unlocked the door, sized the room up, and set his bag down on a low counter. The window was open, with sounds from the street coming from below. He walked over to it, looked down into the street, and saw a car that struck a memory chord—that plume of smoke and the lawn-motor sound. *That's the menace that tried to run me over . . . What did the architect call it again?* Trabant.

Shutting the window and frowning, he turned around, surprised to hear a voice behind him, coming from a chair in the corner by the door. A figure was seated in the chair in the shadows.

The voice continued, repeating itself, "Mr. Dare, Titus Dare, the famous architect?"

"Yes," he said apprehensively. "Who are you, and how did you get in my room?"

"Alan Stecker, US government. Was waiting downstairs, but best not to be seen sitting around for too long."

"Sure. Better to hide out in my room?" Titus quipped. "And how do I know you are who you say you are?"

Ignoring his question but pulling out an identification badge that revealed a holstered pistol under his jacket, the man said, "Welcome to West Berlin, our little experimental museum of the Cold War. I am here to talk about your visit and your project."

Titus looked at Stecker to see if his appearance matched his expectation of what a secret agent might look like. He was square-jawed like a football quarterback but with a certain darkness around his sunken eyes. His manner was casual as he sat in the chair in the hotel room, but it was obvious he could dissolve into the background on a moment's notice.

"How do you know about my project?"

"Well, I'm sort of in the intelligence-gathering game, and besides, it's not necessarily a secret."

"Intelligence . . . Does that mean you're CIA, FBI, Secret Service, or something?"

Ignoring his question again, this time with a dismissive shake of his head, the man said, "Your project has become sort of a diplomatic football, which you may or may not realize. It surprised us they had contacted you directly about the project, given your recent circumstances at home, with your divorce from your wife and retreat from your office."

Titus returned both a puzzled and distressed look.

Stecker continued, "The East has been allowed control of

this thing, your project, since your absence, as a political-politeness gesture to them on our part, since the West was taking the lead on the design competition and the East is responsible for the construction part. For some reason, it has become important to them for you to be here, enough to contact you while you were on your little pause from life. Any idea why the outreach now?"

Titus responded, "Not really. Just a phone call inviting me here. Nothing out of the ordinary for an architect to meet on site about a project."

"Maybe. Maybe not. It is high profile, given the East versus the West aspect, you know.

"It was a phone call to my office, what is left of it," Titus said firmly. "I was . . . I am sort of a high-profile architect, so maybe it is the public-relations aspect if the project has been pushed forward by the East."

Titus was trying to think back about any other aspects that may have warranted other motives and could not help conjecturing about Cold War suspicions. He continued. "Forgive me, but the East-West, spy versus spy, distinction escapes me. Who is the East, considering I am not sure who the West is here? And how am I sure where you sit on the matter?"

"I am from the West, to be sure," replied Stecker.

"I didn't know the US government was involved in my project. It was the builder, Berlin Tor GmbH, who sponsored the competition."

"You have to remember this is Berlin," Stecker said. "Berlin Tor, they were the sponsors in name as a third party between the East and West. Behind them are representatives of the East and West and their technical teams. Not sure why they didn't just proceed without you, given your distraction at home. On the other hand, it is high profile, and it would have been a little curious not to have the main creative ego type present, I suppose."

Titus countered, "I like to think they picked the design in the competition because it was the best design and not for my ego, my reputation. Did you guys influence the outcome of the design competition somehow?"

"That is a very noble thought about the best design winning and quite a compliment that we might have been able to rig a design competition. But in Berlin, buildings are political first and foremost, with the architects typically playing along. Remember the ghosts of Berlin, Albert Speer, among others? Remember, you're surrounded by the enemy, or at least an unsympathetic power to the irritant of West Berlin. There is, however, something that makes you or your design important to the process that we are not quite sure of, since you have been summoned here with a certain urgency that did not go through normal channels."

"You never answered me as to why you're here in my room. So, are you a spy or something?" probed Titus.

"Would you like to see my pen, which is also a camera? Let's just say I'm an interested party, courtesy of your government. Besides, your project is in the US sector of West Berlin, a new building right at the border crossing between East and West, where our tanks and their tanks faced each other down." He paused and smiled. "Location, location, location."

Stecker continued, "It is a building for trade cooperation and glasnost with shared offices for a model of East-West cooperation. Which means the place will be full of spies and bugs, as you might imagine. With both sides planting bugs, a perfect breeding ground for all sorts of cockroach behavior."

Titus gave him a blank stare, starting to wonder if there was some Berlin humor thing he was missing.

"Let me put it more directly," Stecker said. "Your building is ground zero for spooks, despite the building being a diplomatic and cross-border peace pipe."

"Spooks?"

"Intelligence agents, ghosts of Berlin history running around a Cold War," Stecker said dryly.

"So, do laser beams come out of your watch?" asked Titus

sarcastically, getting more impatient by the second.

"No, don't be silly, just some radio-tracking chips." Stecker smiled, then looked at his watch. "What I would like you to do is keep an eye out for anything that seems not right with the building or anyone from the East taking a special interest in your visit. Here is my card." He withdrew one from his shirt pocket and handed it to Titus. "You can reach me at any time of the day or night. I'll see you tomorrow. Get some sleep. Big day tomorrow."

With that, he stood and moved to the door.

Titus asked, "I don't know my schedule. What's happening tomorrow?" he asked.

But Stecker had already left the room.

Titus locked the door behind him and looked around the room. It matched the hotel lobby in aspirations of luxury accommodation with the blandness of concrete as a design feature.

He walked back to the window. There was a long line of lights in the distance. He then looked down and could see Stecker walking down the street. A car's headlights came on, and Titus recognized it, again, as one of those cars, a Trabant. It had been idling but now drove off, seemingly trailing Stecker. Titus turned from the window and sat down in the lounge chair next to the window, with the curtains blowing into the room. He heard a car backfire in the background. *Car needs a muffler tune-up or a gun muzzle silencer*, he thought, with an image in his mind of the Trabant assassinating Stecker.

He closed his eyes, and the weariness of his trip got the better of him. He dreamed of walking on top of a wall in a cloudy mist, catching his balance with every step. He looked down on either side and then looked up and ahead of him. His ex-wife was there, in a glow of mist, standing on the same wall in the distance. He looked down along the path of the wall and, despite the risk of falling, started to move quickly, almost running, straight to his wife.

He reached out with one hand, with the other hand helping to maintain his balance, like a gymnast, and then reached forward with both arms to embrace her. But she smiled and turned to go, her image dissolving into the air. Titus stumbled in his reaching out to her, lost his balance, leaned from side to side, and then fell to his knees to steady himself. He looked down on either side as he wobbled there on top of the wall.

Another car exhaust backfired, louder than the first, waking him from his dream.

He shook off his short nap and looked around the hotel room to confirm where he was. He looked at the bed and thought about sleep. Looked toward the window and thought about Berlin. Sleep or intrigue? He turned to the mirror in the room, straightened up his appearance, grabbed the room key from the desk, and headed out of the room into the corridor.

Titus exited the hotel entrance door after nodding to the front desk clerk. She called out, "Do you need a taxi?"

"No, I will find one," he said, thinking about his last experience. "Just going to take a walk. Which way is the Berlin Wall?"

She made a circular gesture in every direction and smiled weakly. Titus thought, *I guess it is sort of a joke when you are surrounded by a concentration camp wall.*

He stepped down to the street in front of the hotel. It was afternoon, and he started to walk toward what appeared to be a busier street, based on the amount of light and noise. As he walked, he had the sense of someone following him, but when he turned around, he saw nothing suspicious. Just a holdover from the visit by Stecker. No one was tailing him, except maybe that one car back there, which was moving slowly in the distance behind him. He shook it off and kept walking, but once again, he felt the same sense of being followed. He turned and noticed that the car was moving closer, and beyond the headlights, he could see a plume of smoke coming from the rear. A Trabant.

Not one of those things again. He turned back around and kept walking.

He heard the engine noise become louder, and he started to

walk faster to the corner, where he could see other car traffic. His fast walk now broke into more of a jog with a constant glance over his shoulder as the Trabant seemed to be edging up onto the sidewalk.

That thing is trying to kill me. Titus broke out into a full run to the corner, with the Trabant now right behind him. Finally, he reached the corner and made a quick turn down the intersecting busy main street, and the Trabant roared past him, back onto the street and across the street, disappearing in a cloud of smoke.

Titus breathed deeply, in and out. *Berlin is full of surprises, in particular, and a particular type of car that seems to want to hit me.* He shrugged. *Better than buildings falling down on me, I suppose.*

Looking down the main street, he saw a line of pale-yellow taxicabs all idling.

He approached one of the taxicabs and roused the driver from the passenger-side window. "Can you take me to the Wall . . . the Mauer? The Berlin Wall," Titus asked.

The taxi driver gave him a puzzled look, and then both the driver and Titus recognized each other.

"Aacch, my friend, you are still here," said the driver with a smile and then a frown. "Why would you want to go there?"

"Yes, I am still here," replied Titus, thinking, "I want you to take me somewhere along the Berlin Wall where it is the most interesting, the best tourist view of the Wall."

"That sounds, how you say, crazy. We have schoene castles with walls, as you like, and churches too. Schloss Charlottenburg, Gedaechtniskirche, Café Metropole?"

"Maybe on my next taxi ride," Titus said. "Maybe crazy, but you see, I'm an architect, and walls are sort of interesting to me as an architect."

"Buildings are better, Herr Architekt."

"I know. I have a building here, but now I would like to see the Wall."

"Spandau Prison has walls. Walls cause problems. Maybe you are crazy?"

"So I see, especially with trying to get a taxi ride. Let me start my tour with the Wall first, then maybe on to the castles, churches, and prisons. I am sure we will find each other next time for that castle tour."

"Okay, Herr Architect. You are the chef," the driver said.

"Chef?"

"The boss."

Titus nodded and climbed in, and the taxicab started off on its way through numerous streets. Titus gazed out of the window, noticing the surrounding scenery had begun to reduce to a more austere and desolate place. The later it became, the darker things got. The taxicab slowly turned down a street that was completely dark, except for the floodlights in the distance. The taxi driver stopped the car, rested back in his seat, and pointed out through the windshield. Titus looked out through the car window, puzzled as to what there was to see in the darkness. All he could really see was a sharp, white-painted edge of a solid barrier about twelve feet high. Titus leaned forward in his seat to see better, and the taxi driver reinforced the direction in which Titus should look, his pointed finger stressing that there was something to see.

Titus opened the car door, stepped out of the taxicab, and walked in the direction of where the driver was pointing. He looked back, confused, at the driver, who pointed again, indicating for him to go to the left or right.

Frustrated now, Titus called out, "So where is the Wall?"

The driver responded with a more vigorous gesture now, straight ahead.

Titus turned and walked first to the left and then to the right, and he could see now that the solid barrier of the Wall came to a sharp but clumsy acute angle, so it could not be seen as a solid barrier, just as a vertical line disappearing into the darkness on both sides with a glow of lights above it.

What a bizarre alignment, thought Titus, *shaped by streets and politics into a sharp point that makes no sense.* Turning back to the taxi driver, he said, "You cannot see it at all."

"That is the point. Alzo, no charge, free ride courtesy of the two Berlins." The driver then backed up and drove away, shaking his head and laughing.

Titus was at first surprised at being abandoned there but then found a certain comfort in the stillness. He waved a military-like salute toward the taxicab and started walking along one side of the wall toward a wooden platform with steps that he could see in the distance, thanks to the glow of the overhead lights.

Focused on the platform ahead, he did not notice his shadow in front of him, growing until the wavering of the shadow was matched by the sound of a motor behind him—a sound that was now becoming all too familiar. He turned to look over his shoulder; the car headlights were rapidly approaching.

Another killer cartoon car. Titus turned back toward the wood platform and ran as the Trabant bore down on him. He reached the platform and jumped onto the stairs as the car veered toward him and then back onto the street past the platform.

Climbing to the top of the platform, Titus watched the red taillights of the car disappear behind the plume of exhaust. *Strike three*, he thought, trying to find some humor in being nearly run over repeatedly.

From the platform, he looked over the Wall, at its smooth, round top and then down to the ground on his side, at all the colorful graffiti, and then back over the Wall at the lighted area, void of any sense of place, like it had been vacuumed of life. Except he now noticed a guard walking, presumably an East German, with a machine gun and, appropriately, a German Shepherd dog. Titus could see the layers of barriers, of barbed wire and smooth sand and then more barbed-wired fence. He could now see a very crude rectangular guard tower across from him, critically lacking any architectural sensibility, sort of refreshing from his viewpoint, compared to all the ambitions of some of his fellow architects to make themselves famous, to demonstrate their ability to visually masturbate out their genius.

A flash from the guard tower brought him back from his rumination. He realized that a guard had just taken his photograph, and now the guard was looking at him through binoculars. Titus was not sure if he should turn away or wave. He decided a smile was a nonconfrontational, diplomatic response. The guard took another photograph and then picked up his phone.

I hope he is calling his wife. Titus stepped down from the platform, looked cautiously both ways, and walked back the way he had come into the darkness of the night.

Behind him, the headlights of a car pushing out of the darkness behind him started slowly moving. Out of instinct, he started walking faster, and the car followed, keeping to his pace. It then accelerated and drove past him, just missing him.

Curious that it was not a Trabant this time, he thought. *First, spooks and then being run over by a symbol of East German pride and now not a Trabant. What next?*

He decided to just walk back to the hotel. *No more taxicabs for today. Just keep my eyes open for my tin can four-wheeled shadow.*

Titus found his way back to the hotel, looking up and down the street before entering the front door. As he entered, the receptionist smiled and waved to him.

"Did you have a good tour tonight to Berlin?" she asked. "What did you see?"

"I visited your Berlin Wall."

"Why that? There are so many other sights here in Berlin."

"Just out of curiosity. Walls are interesting to an architect," Titus said with conviction.

"Na ja, not so, to someone living inside of one. Herr Dare, you have a message." She pulled out an envelope and handed it to Titus.

"A letter? Thank you. I mean, danke."

Titus moved to the side of the hotel lobby and read the note:

Herr Titus Dare, Please to meet us at the construction trailer at the construction site between Friedrichstrasse and Mauerstrasse tomorrow morning at 0900 Uhr. Berlin Tor GmbH

Titus nodded to the receptionist and headed to the elevators. *I hope there are no more surprises tonight*, he thought, feeling quite weary. Once in the room, after checking for any visitors, with the note in his hand, Titus pulled out a set of drawings for his project and unrolled the drawings on the desk in his room. The site plan indicated the footprint of his building, which sat right on the Wall like a large Arc de Triomphe as a portal between East and West, the Berlin Tor. He ran his finger along the line of the Wall, lifting his finger at the building edge and setting it back down at the other end of the building. He flipped the set of drawings to a building elevation and repeated the same gesture, then tapped right through the open gateway center of the building. *Well, this will be an interesting day tomorrow. Hopefully, one that focuses on architecture and not dodging those odd cars.*

THE WALL

Chapter Four

The next morning, bright and sunny, Titus headed out of the hotel lobby to the street and walked along a crosswalk in front of the hotel with the sudden realization that a Trabant was idling in a cloud of smoke across the street. Feeling refreshed by the morning air, he gave the car a concerned look as it revved up its engine. He hailed a taxicab and climbed in, expecting to see his usual taxi driver, and indeed, a familiar voice greeted him.

"Hallo again, my architect friend. How was your visit at the Wall? Did you make friends with her?"

"I am working on it," he said, and under his breath, "if I do not get run over first."

"Wohin, where to this time? Perhaps a castle?"

Titus pulled out the note from last night from his pocket and tried his best phonetic pronunciation. "Friedrichstrasse and Mauerstrasse. Mauer, does that not mean 'wall'?"

"See, your German is already getting better. Different Mauer, that one from 1-7-0-0, not 1-9-6-3. An early one was torn down. This one here," he said as he pointed out the window, "she is still here."

The taxicab continued on its way and pulled to a stop at some construction trailers, which were backed up by a linear white strip of the Wall that continued on in both directions as far as Titus could see into the distance.

The taxi driver was looking in the direction of a group of men standing in front of the trailers. As Titus exited the taxicab, the driver said, "It looks like they are waiting for you. Auf Wiedersehen, na ja, we say here in Berlin, 'Tschuss.' You must pay this time, today."

Titus offered him once again the playing card fan of US dollars, and the driver pulled out the dollar bills in sequence.

Titus quipped, "I am trusting you," to which the driver replied, "You cannot trust anyone in Berlin, East or West," and off he drove with a wave.

Titus surveyed the construction site and noted a group of men at the cluster of construction trailers and an overhead boom crane that was mirrored by a similar crane on the east side, both with a respective German flag, identical except for the emblem on the east one. He walked up to the trailer, held up a *wait-a-minute* finger to the group of men, walked over to the Wall, and put his hand on the surface. He expected it to be cold from a political Cold War perspective, but the sun hitting it had warmed it up. He patted it, looked at the round top and the angled foundation base to size it up as if it were an opponent, and then headed back to the group of men. One of them approached Titus in greeting. He was dressed like an architect, all in black, with the requisite architect's briefcase and designer wristwatch.

"Good morning, Herr Dare. I am Herr Schmidt, Schmidt, if you like, the local project manager for your project, from the West. I trust you had a good trip to Berlin."

"Yes," Titus paused, "I think so. Interesting, for sure." *Especially when it is life-threatening.*

"I, we would like to introduce you to some of the participants for the construction team. Herr Belsen is our construction specialist, Herr Brock is the structural engineer, Herr Schlesinger the excavator . . . and Mr. Stecker is our special liaison," Schmidt said, pointing to each of the team.

Titus shook hands with each of the men in a formal manner, with a longer handshake with Stecker, the uninvited guest from his hotel room yesterday. Titus acknowledged him with an extra quick nod and then thought that might be some form of spy betrayal. Schlesinger, the excavator, had a different aura about him with a large full head of grey hair and chiseled, weathered facial features, what Titus might have called Prussian, if he knew what that actually meant.

Schmidt continued. "We will be going over to the East, where the project planning main office has been set up. There are some design issues they would like to discuss, hence the request for you to come to Berlin . . . but we are not sure what that means right now. The only thing we know is there is also an issue apparently with some building foundations in the way."

They all entered the trailer, and Schmidt moved to a scale model of Titus's building on the site. While it had been a lengthy time period since the time of designing the building to now, the drawings and perspective rendering were no match for the sensation of seeing the scale model of the building while in a construction trailer on the site next to the Wall. It was indeed a "triumphal arch" in design, with an arched opening elevated above the ground floor through the building from West Berlin to East Berlin. It interrupted the Wall in its length and actually made it seem quite harmless.

As they gathered around the scale model, Schmidt said, "It is an ausgezeichnet, excellent design. Finally, something that makes the Wall make sense, if that is possible. Simple and direct with an opening in it, like our Brandenburger Tor, but more like a hole that has been carved through, if you will. An opening in the Wall, symbolic only, yes, but that is important. One day, that symbolism will give way to a true opening, we only hope."

Looking around the group of men, Titus solemnly spoke. "Thank you for your kind words. I am glad to be here and to see this project move forward."

Schmidt acknowledged Titus's words with a nod. "Our visit

this morning to the east side of the Wall is the first real dialogue we, from the West, have had on the project. The reason for you," gesturing to Titus, "to come here would be considered normal as the architect of a project. As you know, and for Herr Dare's information, our friends, comrades in the East have control over the construction of the project. However, there is some urgency about their outreach to you. We have asked, but they have only said it is a design issue that requires your input. . . and the foundation issue I mentioned. And now they are intending on a foundation-setting ceremony immediately. That is an important symbolic gesture, especially here in Germany, where it is an honor to be involved. It all makes sense and no sense, in a way, but this is Berlin, perhaps the schizophrenia capital of Europe," Schmidt finished, shrugging his shoulders.

Titus, noting the group's focus on himself, said, "I am just glad the project is going ahead, and I appreciate all your interest and support here in Berlin. And . . . I would not be surprised by anything here in Berlin based on my visit so far."

Schmidt looked quizzical but affirmed the observation. "Na, gut, they are waiting for us. Do you have your passport? We need to go through the checkpoint."

The group exited the construction trailer and made their way to what appeared to be a makeshift checkpoint, an odd mixture of steel, glass and cement panels, through the Wall. Each held out their identification papers to a stern-looking East German guard, who performed a rigid formal inspection of the document.

On inspection of Titus's passport, the guard waved his hand in a "stop" motion and went into the adjoining partitioned area with windows and engaged in a conversation with an even more stern-looking officer, who picked up the phone and made a call. As the officer spoke on the phone, Titus noticed that the officer's demeanor came to erect attention, and with several affirmative nods of his head, he put the phone back in its cradle. With a short nod to the inspection guard, the officer looked at Titus through the window. The inspection guard returned and waved Titus through the line with a friendly but somewhat knowing smile.

A member of the visiting group, Stecker, the man from Titus's hotel room, was behind Titus, and as Titus looked over his shoulder, he could see that the inspection guard held up his hand again. Titus turned to wait for Stecker, who was the last of the group. Once again, there was a consultation with the officer in the partitioned area. A longer discussion ensued, and by that time, Schmidt had returned to the checkpoint exit to see where Titus was.

Stecker gestured to Titus to continue on. "I will be with you in a moment. Go on ahead. You are the guest of honor."

Titus headed out the exit door and, accompanied by Schmidt, to a trailer on the other side of the Wall, where construction activity had already started on the foundation excavation for the new building long its perimeter.

As they headed to the construction trailer, Titus looked back closely at the Wall. Waving a hand to Schmidt, Titus walked to the Wall, away from the group, which caused a stir with a nearby East German guard, who tightened his grip on his gun and stepped forward.

Schmidt motioned to the guard that there should be no concern. Titus stepped up close to the Wall and put his hand on the surface, first testing its hardness and then feeling it lightly with a soft touch. It was cold and damp but still the same wall as the other side. Titus turned back and noticed the stern look on Schmidt's face and the soldier's tense posture. He picked up his pace and headed back to the trailer, up the trailer stairs, followed closely by Schmidt.

The group inside the trailer looked at Titus. It was a mixture of his group from the West and new faces. He studied the new faces in the group from the East, trying to discern what their roles might be. A woman among them caught his eye, and she seemed to be just as focused on his eyes. Beyond the group was a scale model of his building, similar to the one in the other construction trailer that they had come from, over on the other side of the Wall.

A more distinguished and self-assured man stepped forward from the group. "Ahh, Mr. Titus, welcome to East Berlin. We are so happy you are here. I am Herr Johann, the project manager for this side. Herr Schmidt, Herr Belsen, Herr Brock, Herr Schlesinger, all willkommen. Ahh, and Mr. Stecker, back again," he said as Stecker entered the trailer, looking a little ruffled.

Herr Johann's appearance was a mix of a design professional and stiff bureaucrat with a touch of rawness around the edges.

The man called Johann continued, "From my side, this is Herr Oster, our Bauleiter, ich meine, construction manager, Herr Sicher, the safety and security manager, and Fraulein Westhoff, our architect for the project. She will be your main liaison for the project and will work most closely with you."

That sounded a little deliberate to Titus, but he assumed it might be just the use of English. Handshakes were exchanged all around after the introductions. Titus did register that the woman was expressing a definite warmness in her smile and handshake. He noticed her clothes, in particular, as they looked like a soldier-fashion version of civilian clothes - a tight collar and tight pants, like riding breeches, cut to the female body and tucked into military-style boots. She had very clear blue eyes, high cheekbones and blond hair in a tight, braided bun at the back of her head. She looked familiar somehow with it finally registering that the familiarity was to his wife's face.

Titus's assessment was interrupted by Herr Sicher, who motioned for her and the group to move farther into the trailer.

Herr Johann gestured to a large table. "If you please . . . please sit down."

The group all sat at a table with bottles of water and glasses at each place. Titus recalled images he had seen of international political negotiations, and this scene reminded him of those pictures.

"Erstens, Herr Dare, and our West comrades, we are happy that you are here and that this building is starting again. Most important here is that there are, however, some things that require Herr Dare's input on the project, as the architect," said Herr Johann, and he stood up near the scale model.

He gestured toward the model with a wave of his hand. "There is one fundamental change which is not small, but the project will not proceed without it. We feel it keeps the building design itself intact. We understand your competition concept of the project being a Tor, a visual gateway, as per the intention of the project, but some things have changed. And an acceptable compromise to have the project built is necessary. We feel there needs to be a change, for the positive and for the project to proceed," Herr Johann concluded in a polite but firm tone.

He gently picked up the building model and turned it 90 degrees so that it straddled the Wall instead of being a gateway through the Wall.

Titus looked at the scale model, then looked around the room to see if this was some form of prank as part of his welcome, like a scene from the movie *The Fountainhead*. He felt a familiar nervous sensation from his previous emotional collapse before this trip to Berlin—one of not being in control of the situation. He was used to the challenges of design problems and client personalities and even challenges to his capabilities and professionalism. Under normal conditions, he would reach inside himself and find self-assurance from his work. It was not new for design changes to be requested and modifications made, but this was drastic, even under the strange circumstances of the political shadow of where his building was located, between East and West. This was different, and Titus was uncertain about his course of action. Artistic outrage or technical design logic?

Titus's mind started with the former route. *But you cannot do that. That is crazy. Is this a joke?* Ultimately, however, he chose design logic as his actual expressed approach. "My original design interrupts the Wall but becomes part of it and provides a gateway through it. That is the symbolism of the whole design, a ceremonial passage through the Wall, indicating a promise of cooperation. You are straddling the Wall like some clumsy . . ."

Herr Johann interrupted, "It is a bridge across the two sides, a symbolic handshake over the Wall. Different symbolism but the same message of cooperation."

"While it might be a bridge across and over the Wall, the idea was to cross the wall with people and open cooperation, not the building. Maybe it is a handshake across the fence of two neighbors, but it is not the open door of cooperation that is the design intention," stressed Titus.

"A very noble gesture, and no doubt why you won the competition. But the change was requested by the East, ich meine, by us because it is currently not possible to remove the section of the Wall for the construction. So, to proceed with this design, we had to turn the building 90 degrees."

Stecker cut in just then, possibly sensing an escalation and wanting to protect Titus. "Beyond the aesthetic changes, this is a major change in the political and security aspects. From our side, this is a breach of our idea and agreement for the project. We cannot allow this."

Titus added, "I cannot see a positive aspect to this. I do not care about the politics. It is the integrity of the design."

Again, in a firm manner, Herr Johann replied, "It is necessary and advantageous to all. This way, the East gets a part to build, and the West gets a part, and the rooms in between are still meeting rooms between the sides, as you originally designed."

Titus became visibly upset and started to pace in front of the scale model, with his chin lifted, looking at the ceiling. Stecker approached Titus and whispered to him, "Over my dead body will this happen. This is not acceptable from our side nor in terms of surprise decisions. Let me make a call from our trailer, on the other side," and then addressing Herr Johann, he said, "Excuse me, Herr Johann, entschuldigung." Stecker quickly left the trailer. The ensuing awkward moment was interrupted by Herr Johann. "Now, we see it as a bridge instead of a gateway and equally poetic as your original design. Most importantly, construction can begin promptly, as we are not ready for the Wall to be interrupted, or removed by construction. Security is much better with each side having their own building, and the East has agreed to coordinate the construction of the bridge between, a bridge of détente, if you wish."

On his own now, Titus countered, "With all respect, that changes the whole building. It is not the intention and no offense meant to you, but an insult to the building and my design."

"We of all people are sensitive to that, and we hold our architects in high esteem here, but as you may recall, you won an *ideas* competition. There was a waiver you signed about the competition sponsors having the right to alter the project as necessary. We do not like to make a large change any more than you, but that is the political reality, of cooperation."

Titus looked around the room for some understanding of his position. "With all due respect again, the building is supposed to be like this." He picked up the building model, turned it, and pushed it back down, flattening the cardboard Wall on the model that was in the way. Admiring the result, Titus turned back to the group. "Herr Dare, you must understand, and as you know from the competition brief, it asked for the building to be a gesture for cooperation and reunification. It is a trade center. You saw it as a gateway, and for the greater good, it has become a bridge. Different words, same building, different orientation, same purpose," stressed Herr Johann, maintaining his composure but trying to force his point.

Titus thought his gesture with the building needed a punch and hoped that his artistic integrity and indignation might work. "I will not have anything to do with it."

Herr Johann countered, "It is very important for the East project sponsor that you *do* have something to do with it. It is important for us and West Berlin and *you* as the architect. At another level, it was your design that convinced both sides that this is the correct way to bring the two sides together. We ask that you understand our position and hopefully agree to participate in the foundation cornerstone ceremony that will take place three days from now. If you can cooperate, you can expect to receive other work here, which I am sure you could use . . . especially at this time in your career," he said, sounding a bit threatening but then softening with a pause. "I am sure this project will be the starting point for a long career here."

Titus felt his pride welling up. "If I had known this, I never would have come."

"All we are asking is that you spend a little time with us in the East and refresh yourself with the current circumstance of the project . . . and the people involved. Can you do that? It is very important . . . for us and for you and your work."

The exchange of words was interrupted by Stecker, who was standing in the doorway of the trailer. "Titus, can I have a word with you outside?" Titus approached, and Stecker took Titus by the arm and guided him outside. They walked a short distance from the trailer, and Stecker faced Titus. "Well, I did not see that one coming."

"Isn't that your job?"

"We do not really track architectural design, just spies and saboteurs." Stecker shot a sidelong glance back at the trailer. "Look, I know you artistic types are protective of your work, but I'm going to have to ask you to play along. I spoke with my director, and he thinks we need to see where this goes. As I said before, in your hotel room, there is something in play here, and your help is needed. Consider it a civic duty to the free world."

"I am not a spy, just an architect," replied Titus, becoming annoyed with the request.

"Appreciate that," Stecker replied, "but your cooperation will help immensely, and it will be also very much appreciated by the US government. How would you like to design the new embassy here?"

"I am not for sale, either to them or to you," Titus asserted.

"Everybody has a price, especially in my business. Let me try another route. If you want to protect your design, no matter how it is turned, you will humor the situation and see what you can find out. No risk, just try to see if you can find out why they are turning it. Could be harmless, just one of those things that happens in architecture, change in scope, I think you call it. We have our thoughts on it—that something is causing the shift besides the political-architectural excuse they gave. Look at it as an opportunity, not a problem. That's what architects always say when they are in trouble. Anyway, you creative guys like to solve problems, right?"

"I came for an architectural project, not an undercover assignment. And this is not a change in scope. It is a gutting of the whole concept. Basic attack on the design, worse than Pearl Harbor."

Stecker paused for a moment, then posed a counter-thought. "Actually, your attitude might be exactly what I'm looking for. I need your cooperation for our side, and I am counting on your stubbornness to buy us more time. See if you can get any information from the girl architect. You two seemed to connect there in the trailer. Maybe swap some creative juices," he said with a slight smirk, "and we can get your building back the way you want it, as you designed it."

"That only works for James Bond, where his charm works its magic on the female villain," Titus said with a shake of his head.

"Won't hurt to try. She is sort of a looker, in my spyglass, for a comrade. What would a trip to Berlin be without a little intrigue? Let me do a little undercover work while I am over here in the East, while you are playing architect," Stecker said, trying to lighten up the exchange.

"This is not my idea of being an architect nor a typical day in the office, playing architect, as you would call it. More like an architect's worst nightmare—a major surprise at the first on-site construction meeting, surrounded by guards with machine guns."

Stecker laughed. "Berlin, I mean, the Berliners are not typical, always remember the split personality. It is a challenge, just like a design, I suppose. But remember, you can trust no one to be as they seem. Always two sides here."

"I can't see the other side. And what about trusting you?" Titus shot back.

"I can . . . see both sides from my side, that is," he said. "And, as I saw it, the girl architect in the trailer seemed to be very interested in you. See what you can do with her, find out what's going on."

"Look, I have enough professional … and personal issues to not be blind-dating a Communist architect, who, according to you, might not be trustworthy."

"Just have an open mind and, better yet, open eyes. Maybe you can convince them to turn the building," Stecker said and started to turn back to the trailer. Just then, the door swung open, with Herr Johann in the doorway. "Here we go," Stecker muttered.

Without a word to Johann, Titus and Stecker returned to the construction trailer, and Stecker addressed the group. "Mr. Dare has thought it over, and he has agreed to listen and work with your design."

Titus gave Stecker a disapproving glance and then said to the group, "I do not see the point of my involvement at all, but I will listen out of courtesy and out of curiosity for how you think you can still maintain the original design intent." Turning to the female architect Westhoff, he added, "As I have come this far, I am interested to find out about what it is like here in the East."

Herr Johann stepped in on Titus's speech. "Na, Gut. Fraulein Westhoff here is responsible for the architectural changes on the project for the East. Now that Herr Dare has expressed his concern about the changes to the design, I think it would be appropriate if Fraulein Westhoff explained our point of view more."

She cleared her throat and straightened her jacket. "Two things have been given. The first is that your design requires a section of the Wall to be removed, which is still currently a security breach for our government in terms of people wanting to enter into East Berlin without permission."

Titus looked up at the ceiling and then gave Stecker a puzzled look. Stecker seemed to hold his breath, as if expecting an outburst from Titus.

She continued, "This has not been diplomatically resolved as anticipated by the design competition. Secondly, the construction was meant to be a joint effort, and the new design allows each side to build their own part, based on this security issue. The connecting element, therefore, becomes all important, and that is where we are asking you," nodding to Titus, "to work with us on the redesign of the central portion of the building and site plan, as in a bridge instead of an arch. I think we can work this out together." Again, she nodded toward Titus, but this time with more of a military delivery, and then a smile. "I look forward to working with such a famous architect."

Titus did not know what to say, and he started to object with his body language and a slight shake of his head, still not accepting the request made of him. He looked around the room at all the men looking back at him, and then he returned to Fraulein Westhoff, who maintained her smile. Stecker gave Titus an encouraging nod.

Titus, still trying to salvage the original design, said to her, "Mr. Johann and you have said something about a bridge instead of a gateway. That is . . . a totally different idea."

Fraulein Westhoff looked at Herr Johann and then back to Titus. "But that is why we want you to work with us on the redesign. If you are like me, a new design project is always the best. Are you like me in that way?" She was putting Titus on the spot in front of all the others in the room. Silence ensued as she waited for a response.

Titus shifted his weight on his feet, looked at the floor, paused, looked up, and decided that now was not the time to throw an artistic tantrum, "My reputation is based on the challenge of new design, as you note, but also not compromising. I can see the bridge aspect, but I am very skeptical. How do you expect this to happen at this point in time?"

Fraulein Westhoff quickly answered the group, "We will work very closely, right away if you like. As said and based on the altered design, the East has the responsibility for building the east side of the building and now also the center section as part of the cooperative construction effort, but we need your design input on the Bruecke, a bridge over the Wall now. It is not a gateway anymore, and the design has to reflect a bridge, between the two Germanies and for the future." Her voice rose with some pride. "While we look at the new design, we have also arranged a visit to our prefabricated, I think that is the correct word, concrete factory where the central bridge span sections will be made. You, Herr Dare, can see what we are . . . what is possible to build. We will then spend some time together on the redesign. I am sure, in your hands, the project will be a better project and improve diplomatic ties. I suggest we spend a little time here, going over the project, and then take a break to visit the factory."

There was a short, awkward pause, which was broken by Herr Johann. "Danke, aah, a little bit of détente. Na, gut. We will leave you beide to work out this."

The group lined up to shake Titus's hand and then filed out of the trailer. Stecker turned and gave him a sly smile. The last man out, whom Titus thought was 'Schlesinger', the excavator, gave him a look of friendly suspicion.

Fraulein Westhoff gestured toward a table with a set of drawings, and she spread the drawings out. Titus flipped through them to see which design was represented in the drawings and nodded approvingly that they were his original design. He then looked at the model with a shake of his head.

She said, "I am sorry for this surprise for you," as she reached in front of him to clear the table in front of them. Titus could not help but catch the strong smell coming from Fraulein Westhoff, or at least from her clothes. She continued. "Herr Dare, may I say what a great honor it is to work with you on this?"

Titus replied, "I am just an architect, like you. How did you get involved with this project?"

"I would like to say it is that I am talented like you. For us here, though, it is a matter of trust . . . and control, especially the closer we get to the Wall. I am safe, a trusted comrade. Trust here, though, is based on control and consequences."

Titus replied with a smile, "Guess I should ask if I can trust you. This whole Cold War is like Antarctica for me, far away and unimportant."

She answered quickly, "Architecture and trust are universal languages. Political boundaries are only temporary statements."

"Politics, however, do make strange bedfellows," Titus quipped and thought about what he had just said as he received a puzzled look from Westhoff. "That probably will not translate very well, even if I spoke German. But your English is very good."

"I think you mean that the Cold War can thaw under the right conditions, oder?"

Titus continued, "You gave as a reason for turning the building that it was necessary due to the Wall not being able to open as a gate. Besides changing the whole idea, it changes the entrances, the foundations, the opening in the middle of the building, and the cost. Any other reasons for turning it? Political ones, perhaps?"

There was a short but awkward pause as no answer came

immediately from Westhoff, until she responded with firmness, "My assignment on this . . . is to work with you to come up with a revised design that is acceptable to everyone. The more I understand about the design and you, the more I can help to persuade you to work with this situation."

"Being persuaded. That is not my strong point," Titus said, returning the stiffness.

"My instructions are to get your agreement."

"I appreciate your honesty and determination. I will keep an open mind, but you can imagine my surprise earlier."

"All I can ask is that we work together, cooperate," Westhoff said in a friendlier tone and turned her attention to the drawings.

They continued to review the drawings with pencils in hand as time lapsed and the daylight outside the trailer shifted toward the afternoon.

Westhoff noticed the time on her watch, "Well, how do you feel about the project now?"

"Truthfully, it is still conceptually wrong, in my mind," Titus said. "I just cannot compromise on it. The only way I can look at it is as a new project. In one sense, that is why I have traveled here, to make a new start after . . ." He paused and changed the subject back to the drawings. "Your thoughts as you have drawn them here are interesting in terms of redesigning the project."

"Are you sure about that, or are you just being polite to me, a fellow architect?"

"Well, what do you think, honestly?" asked Titus, trying to catch the focus of her eyes as a way of convincing her of his sincerity.

Westhoff, seeming slightly embarrassed by the question, changed the subject. "Shall we take a pause and go on the visit to the beton, I mean, concrete factory?"

They exited the trailer and started walking to what appeared to be her automobile. *Oh, good grief,* he thought, as he recognized the car sitting near the trailer as a Trabant. Westhoff proceeded to the driver's door while Titus slowed his steps to size up the Trabant, walking around the automobile and ending at the passenger door.

"Something wrong?" came her voice from inside the automobile.

"Oh, nothing," Titus said, thinking, *These things have been trying to run me over since I arrived here, and now I am sitting in one of them. It was only a matter of time, I suppose.*

"Bitte? Something wrong?"

Once inside, he thought, *No, I'm just a little afraid of cars, killer cars, that is.* But to her, he said, "What is this car type?"

"It is a Trabant, our car for the people," said Westhoff with a thin, partially concealed smile.

"I hope it is safer on the inside than it looks on the outside," Titus said under his breath.

"What do you mean, on the inside? I am a safe driver."

"No doubt. I just have a way of having trouble with certain cars." Harder to hit me if I'm on the inside, though. With a creak of the passenger door, he stepped into the car. Westhoff looked at him, perplexed.

Responding to the look, "Never mind. What is your first name, by the way?"

"Frieda. It means 'peace' in English."

"That is perfect," Titus said to her and then, as he closed his car door, muttered, "Perfectly ironic."

She clearly had not heard the whole comment—which was his intention—and she asked, "Wie bitte? Sorry."

Titus looked out through the windshield. "I'm in the middle of a city that is at the tip of the iceberg of the Cold War, and my tour guide is Peace."

Westhoff looked at him, puzzled at first, then with a smile as the comment sank in. She turned to look straight out the windshield and started the vehicle. Titus reacted with a jolt to the loud start-up sound of the car and then ducked his shoulders at the subsequent backfire, looking around as if someone were shooting at them.

Noticing Titus's reaction, Westhoff laughed. "They are not shooting at you . . . not yet," and she moved the car forward with its two-cycle rattle in a cloud of blue smoke. They drove through the heart of East Berlin. She pointed out some of the historical landmarks of old Berlin and then, with some pride, pointed out a very large, very drab and fascist-looking East Berlin building.

"That is our parliament building, our Volkspalast, the People's Palace. It replaced the old Schloss Berlin, the Berlin Castle, damaged in the war and not a fit symbol for the new East Berlin and its workers."

Titus looked at the building carefully. "Not exactly what I would call a symbol of humanity, of democracy, the Demokratische Deutsche Republik, correct? Pretty stark . . ." and then sensing that his observations were off target, added, "but powerful-looking."

They drove by the Altes Museum, Neues Museum, the Museum Insel, Alexanderplatz, and the Rotes Rathaus. Despite the circumstances, it felt like a sightseeing trip for tourists as she pointed out the car windows, this way and that. They turned down a street that appeared to be a dead end, with the barbed wire of the death strip from the east side of the Wall confronting them.

An East German soldier with a dog walked in front of their car and looked at them, first with curiosity and then suspicion. The somewhat light atmosphere of two sightseeing architects changed in the car. Not meaning to challenge the guard but to get a better look at the Wall, Titus opened the door. The guard now focused his gaze on Titus, and the guard dog started barking at him. As the guard stepped forward, now with a grip on his machine gun, Westhoff reached across the inside of the car and tapped on the passenger-side window, signaling for Titus to get back in the car. Titus kept his eyes on the guard as he slid back into his seat. She backed up the car in lockstep with the guard's steps forward, and she waved politely as they turned away.

They now proceeded with the drive, without talking, into the outskirts of East Berlin to the factory complex where the concrete building components were to be manufactured. Titus looked out the car window at the grayness and thought about the stare of the guard with the Wall behind him.

Trying to break the awkwardness of silence, Titus said, "So this is what East Berlin looks like outside the central city. Very different from the West areas I saw on the train trip."

"I would not know. We do not travel easily to the West," Westhoff replied with a certain remnant of stiffness.

"I am not sure how well I travel to the East. Things did not go well in the construction trailer back there with the group."

Westhoff softened. "It is my responsibility to make you see

things differently for the better, to cooperate. Despite the closed society you might see, I have an open mind and my orders . . . my responsibility is to keep your mind open. Through architecture and my . . . showing you a new way. A creative mind is an open one, oder?"

"I can see why you are my . . . handler, but this is a twist for me. In the West, my unwillingness to compromise is somewhat valued, maybe even considered noble as an architect. Here, I am also considered close-minded and maybe lacking in creativity . . . but need to have an open mind. A little schizophrenic for me but . . ." Titus paused.

"Wie bitte? Scizophree?"

"Schizophrenic, it means a split personality. I think my mistake was designing one unified building. I should have designed twin buildings, one for you and one for me," Titus said with a sly smile and hand gesture indicating two sides of an object.

They pulled up to a factory building, exited the car, and entered the factory. It was a drab, gray, metal-clad building, possibly from before World War II, and it was equally drab and dark inside with exposed light bulbs hanging in rows.

Looking around, Titus observed, "This is an old factory. I would have thought this would be a newer operation for the building."

"In the East, we have to make use of what we have, over and

over. The National Socialists used this for making their concrete bunkers, on a large scale. The pieces of our Wall were made here as well," Westhoff said with some reluctance in her voice.

They walked along the concrete formwork pouring troughs, industrial manufacturing machines, and overhead crane lines.

"Here are the . . . die Schalung," Westhoff said, pointing around the facility. "I think you call them work forms. How would you call them in English?"

"Casting beds," offered Titus.

She raised her eyebrows. "Beds, as in sleeping?"

"Yes, like that, but for concrete."

"We have prepared for the beams that will connect the two halves of the building already. This is the first test cast to see if our technique will produce the right quality and strength . . . stiffness. They are set up for two meters deep for the span over the Wall."

"That is about six feet deep, right? Just over my head," Titus said, gesturing with his hand and then looking around. "What is that over there?"

"That is the Funderstein, cornerstone for the project, just poured today, per the schedule and ceremony," she said as they walked over to it together and looked at the inscription on the stone: *Eine Bruecke fuer die Voelker.*

Titus tried to pronounce the words and turned to Westhoff. "What does that mean?"

"I think in English it would be *A Bridge for the Peoples*."

"Pretty presumptuous considering the surprise attack on my building just this morning," Titus observed.

"Wie bitte? I do not understand."

"Looks like my compromise has been made for me, unless there is another one that says *A Gateway for the Peoples*," clarified Titus staring at the cornerstone.

She smiled awkwardly and looked closer at something at the top of the concrete mold bed, and Titus leaned over to look at it as well. It appeared to be a handprint with part of the wrist showing in the concrete.

Titus looked closer at the handprint. "Someone seems to have proudly signed their work as well. Sort of like the handprints on Hollywood Boulevard, where someone is immortalized in concrete. Children do it in concrete sidewalks all the time."

Westhoff reached out her hand and scratched her finger along the handprint, which seemed to be still soft and wet. "It sticks out, though."

"Odd, in this light," Titus pushed an overhead hanging light in the direction of the top of the cornerstone, "it does look like it's not an imprint, but it's sticking out . . ." He reached out and touched it, then pulled his finger back. "It *is* sticking out, and it is soft! That's strange for concrete."

He grabbed a hammer from a side table and gave the surrounding concrete a tap. It had hardened on the surface but was still pliant below. He then hit the handprint itself, and all the concrete covering it flaked off.

Westhoff screamed and recoiled, "Scheisse! It is a hand!"

Titus, after the initial shock, used the hammer claw to lift up the fingers and saw more concrete move in the area where an arm would be. "Possibly a whole body in there?" he remarked in shock, and then under his breath, hoping to gain some composure, "What is going on? Not a good omen for the cornerstone of a building, *anywhere* . . . and particularly not in Berlin."

"Was is das, under the hand?" Westhoff asked as Titus moved the hammer claw deeper under the fingers.

"It has wires attached to it, like little speakers or a microphone," Titus observed, pulling on the wires which pulled the hand higher. "Shit. I recognize that wristwatch. It's Stecker's spy watch."

Titus's voice was loud enough to attract some unwanted attention, apparently based on voices that were getting louder in the distance.

Westhoff grabbed Titus's arm and pulled him down behind the cornerstone.

"Staatsicherheit Polizei. Stasi. State . . . security . . . police," she whispered. Then she turned around, stood upright for a moment, but then immediately crouched back down. "Stay down. There are police over there. We must not be found here with . . . this." She pointed up at the hand protruding from the foundation-stone.

"Should we not tell them, who we are?" Titus whispered back.

Westhoff gave him a look like he was crazy. "It is best in the East to not know about these things. This is not good for you being here with this."

The voices, now more than one, were getting louder.

"Verdammt. Los, schnell," and she pushed Titus to start moving. And they did, staying in their crouched positions, heading in the opposite direction of the voices. They shuffled between the rows of pre-cast concrete components, staying low until they started in a half-run toward an exit door ahead, Titus now pulling Westhoff with him as he ran faster.

Their movement was hard to keep quiet, and they heard "Halt, halt!" and the sound of boots behind them. The two ran down the last aisle of the factory, hearing another very loud "Halt!" behind them, and then a gunshot ricocheted off the wall next to them. Now, they started to run full stride toward the exit to the outside and to the safety, hopefully, of Westhoff's car.

Once outside, Titus turned and looked back toward the factory door for any signs of pursuit, and then they both jumped into the car, with Westhoff starting the engine. They pulled away in the car, with Titus anxiously looking over his shoulder, hoping not to see their pursuers.

Yet there they were. "Dammit," he said. The men, who wore military uniforms, climbed into an official-looking Trabant, also in military colors, and pulled out behind them in chase.

Off went the two cars in chase down the roads of villages, past industrial buildings and open land. Titus alternated between looking out the rear window and the front windshield, in disbelief that this was really happening. Westhoff had a determined look on her face. He looked at the speedometer; it was at 100 kilometers per hour, which was 60 miles per hour. He shook his head, and the absurdity of the situation overcame the danger, and he started to laugh.

Westhoff gave him a questioning glance. "What is so funny, to laugh? They are chasing us!"

Titus glanced around the car's interior. "These damn cars have been trying to run me over since I got here, and now I am in one, escaping from another one."

His assessment of the situation changed as a gunshot rang out.

"They are shooting at us . . . with guns," was her sharp response coinciding with the sound of another gunshot.

Titus was rattled but still registered the strange conditions in which he was under. "This is not my typical day at the office. How about you?"

Westhoff looked at him again in even more disbelief and then started to laugh.

Titus checked out the speedometer again, still hovering at 100 kilometers per hour . . . *60 mph*, he calculated. *I have never been in a high-speed chase in my life and never dreamed it would be this slow.*

She looked in the rearview mirror, and Titus looked over his shoulder. She had put some distance between her and their pursuers. "I have the advantage of Schwarzmarkt, how you say . . . black market automobile parts." She patted the dashboard. "Better than the government parts."

A large bang brought them back to the reality of the situation and the worry of the moment.

Westhoff looked intently forward. "Happy they are neither good shots nor good drivers." Titus glanced back through the rear car window again—just as a bullet hit the car. "Getting better at the shooting part," he deadpanned.

"We will have to come loose of them. Halt fest!" Westhoff turned the car sharply between two farmhouses and then kept making continuous hard right turns until they ended up *behind* the car chasing them. With the other car unwittingly speeding away from them now, they slowed down.

"How did you know how to do that?" Titus asked as he watched the plume of the other car disappear. He was shocked at Westhoff's skill in shaking their pursuers, and just kept looking forward with hands on his knees.

She turned to him and said, "In the East, we have many skills, from our military service. Staying clear of the police is something we also learn as comrade citizens," and she pulled the car off the road onto a dirt path through a clump of trees and bushes.

"I don't think we can hide from them here, with so few cars on the road," Titus remarked, trying to think ahead.

"Na, there are only a couple of types of cars here, as you can see, and even less colors, so we will not stand out."

She climbed out of the car, found a spot of wet mud, and smeared the mud over the license plates. She then opened the trunk, pulled out a rag, and wiped her hands clean. After throwing the rag back in the trunk, she shut the trunk and got back into the car.

Titus watched her action with interest. "I'm new to this whole Cold War thing, but why are you hiding from your own government?"

"I am supposed to get you to cooperate, and that is hard to do if you are connected to dead spies. . . or you . . . are dead."

"Appreciate that. Where are we going to go now?"

Westhoff stared out the window for some time, then, "I have a private place where I like to go. It is safe."

She pulled back onto the road and traveled slowly, watching out for other car traffic. After a distance, she turned into an area full of trees and pulled up against what appeared to be the Wall again at the end of the lane.

Titus blinked. "Is that the Wall?"

"Ja. But just the Pruefung . . . you would call it 'the test of the design'?"

"You mean the mockup? There was a mockup of the Berlin Wall, for construction testing?"

"Ja, the mockup, as you would say. This is where they . . . tested the original wall design, to see how it . . . funktioniert. They tested here for constructing the wall quickly, the foundation setting, the top of the wall for stopping climbing over the wall, keeping spies from the West out. The concrete for the wall came from the factory we just visited."

"So, this is somewhere safe here, in the shadow of a wall, the Berlin Wall?" Titus asked doubtfully.

"It is, as you say, a personal place for me."

They climbed out of the car, and she led him to a red door in the wall. It was dark where they were standing, under the trees on that side of the wall, and there the shadows closed in on them at the door in the wall.

"This wall has a door?" Titus said, stating the obvious but wondering why exactly the door was there.

"Mine does." Westhoff smiled. "Not as impressive as the gateway of your building."

Titus gazed along the length of the wall in each direction, "No graffiti on the wall here?"

"Wie bitte?" responded Westhoff as she worked on the door's lock. She set her briefcase on the ground so she could get a better angle on the key lock.

"On the west side, the Wall is a mural for artistic expression. Word and pictures, as a way of making it disappear," Titus said.

"On our side, we are not so free to express. But my wall here is anders, different."

She finally unlocked the door and pushed it open, and they entered. A complete surprise greeted Titus as a flood of sunshine hit him. Inside, it was a greenhouse space filled with flowers and sunlight, even though it was shaded on the other side, where they had been standing just moments ago.

"This is amazing, like the Garden of Eden."

"I use it as a greenhouse to grow plants, a place to dream," she said. "The sun hits the wall on this side, and it heats up and gives back the warmth at night. It has a coal oven as well, for those dark days here."

"So where is the Tree of Knowledge," Titus probed, "in your Garden of Eden? You know, from the Bible - Genesis."

"Our state does not encourage belief in old tales of religion," she said.

"It is more a story of a natural state, a paradise before your worker's paradise. Possibly better to have stories about fictional magical trees in the old tales than the reality of machine guns and watchtowers," Titus offered.

Westhoff started to walk him around the greenhouse, and then she gestured for him to sit down on some rather rudimentary garden furniture. There were some statues, partially broken, set up as garden ornaments. He looked at a male and female statue, the two looking at each other, very similar to the first couple from Genesis, "Where are these from?"

"The ruins of Berlin," she replied, "homeless after the war. I gave them a home here."

"Adam and Eve?" queried Titus, examining the statue pair—a man and a woman surrounded by the afternoon light and green plantings.

"The West and the East, perhaps," returned Westhoff.

"Which is which?" Titus asked, enjoying the exchange and relaxing from the previous anxiety of being shot at. "Or better, which one has the forbidden fruit?"

"Both do, in an unfortunate way." Westhoff seemed to recognize that the conversation was becoming about politics and not statuary, and she asked, "Would you like a tea or coffee?"

"How about something more appropriate? Any Russian vodka to wash down the dust from our car chase?"

Westhoff stood up, saying, "I have something better."

She walked across the greenhouse and went behind a curtain at the end, where there appeared to be a kitchen area. Then, his eyes surveyed the entire area. The space had the appearance of interior design with 'found objects,' definitely selected for design sense, but whatever Westhoff could find.

He noticed her briefcase down on the floor, near the garden furniture. A file with his name on a label sticking out of the top of the briefcase was in clear view. It resembled a personnel folder, for intelligence gathering, perhaps, based on the current circumstances, and he looked over to the curtain where Westhoff was to make sure she was not coming out right then.

Titus slipped the folder out carefully with another look toward the curtain and flipped it open to see photographs of himself and his wife, his buildings, and more recent photos of him in Berlin, arriving at his hotel. His mind went to the spy films he had watched where the agent was put into a compromising position, a 'honeytrap' he remembered was what it was called. *Not sure what they could blackmail me with, though. There was a name for that too, 'kompromat'. These two Berlins with spy versus spy in a Cold War is beginning to get to me.*

As he heard a noise coming from the kitchen, he put the folder back into the briefcase, noticing for the first time a pistol tucked in there. He looked up, trying to regain his composure after seeing the gun and wondering why she would have it with her during his visit.

To cover his snooping, he stood up and called out to her, just as she came from behind the curtain, "Is it safe here to speak about your life and politics?"

"Depends on who is listening," she said, carrying two shot glasses and two bottles of clear liquid. "We can always speak our minds, just not what our hearts feel. That is where secrets and betrayal occur. A lover or a friend may not be as they seem."

Titus gestured toward the drinks. "Nectar of the gods? Or truth serum?"

"Wie bitte? Pardon?"

"What is that you have there?" asked Titus, again gesturing to the bottles.

"It is brandy, an apple and a pear flavor," she answered, raising one bottle and then the other.

Titus smiled. "The Biblical scholars cannot decide if it was an apple or a pear from the Tree of Knowledge. The only thing certain is that Eve gave it to Adam."

"You can choose . . . apple or pear?"

"As a shape, I prefer apples," Titus said, reaching for the bottle with the apple on it.

"Then you should try the pear for a change, to keep an open mind." Westhoff offered him the bottle with the pear, instead.

Titus smiled, realizing this was a reference back to his building and the mandated change. She poured him a glass from the pear-flavored bottle and an apple one for herself. She handed the glass to him, and her hand lingered on his. Titus felt a certain warmth in her touch, and he fought to recover his senses and change the subject. He noticed the sun was changing in the greenhouse, and his mind returned to the purpose of his visit to Berlin.

"How did you end up working on this project, really?" Titus queried.

"The project sponsor selected me. I told you I had been specially chosen to work with you for my design sense, my diplomatic skills, and my previous dedication to my work for my country." She shifted, seeming uncomfortable beneath Titus's focused gaze.

"Your English is very good. Is that one of your special skills, for your assignment?" Titus asked, diverting the subject.

"We mostly have learned Russian in my training. My English is different. My father was an American soldier who met my mother in the ruins of Berlin and those conditions," Westhoff said with a softness to her voice.

"I see, so you learned English as a child."

"And then through some prohibited access to television in the West and some of your movies, but also some of our movies about evil capitalists," she said in a teasing tone.

"Speaking of evil capitalists, who is this project sponsor, as you call him here, and why am I so important? They could have just changed things, and maybe I would end up taking my name off the project in an artistic fit, after some attorney letters," Titus said, realizing he had returned to the topic of his project.

"From what I have overheard, the Bauherr—you would call

him a developer, I believe—is a businessman with his brother, a twin. They have connections both in the East and West. I met them only once. They have done their research on you and understand your thinking. They understand it is your design, but they want you to change it. They can be very persuading, er, persuasive."

"But my position, my stubbornness, can only complicate things, so why keep me involved?"

"This is a special project, the design competition and the selection of your design. It is, how you say . . . high profile for both governments, and you have a high profile among architects."

"Makes it even more complicated if they are counting on my recent reputation."

"Na ja, with the Wall, there are even more complications as it passes through the heart of Berlin—many spirits in Berlin here, much more difficult to deal with than us, the living."

"How do you really feel about the design?"

"To be truthful, unter vier Augen . . . between our four eyes, I liked it the way it was. I understand the change, and the Politik seems to be stronger on this. I think there is something else that is going on, why the change was so sudden. There are existing foundations in the way, which is why just turning the project is currently halted, and a solution from you is being discussed. They feel they need your approval, your agreement, for the changes to overcome the difficulties.”

"That baffles me, I must say," Titus said, focusing on her and changing the subject. "What is your life like here?"

"I am sure it is like your life—air, sunshine sometimes, work," she said, gesturing, then becoming more pensive. "Or maybe not the same. Life is simple here, and I have what I need."

"What about your freedom?"

Westhoff paused for a moment. "I am lucky here, with this," pointing to the greenhouse space again, "and my work. What is it like over there, with you?"

"Free to be stubborn and to make mistakes, and consequently not simple for me or people close to me."

"You are still married, no?"

"Some would say to my work," Titus said with a shrug. "I was, at one time, married. Surprised you did not know. I thought you said you . . . they had done their research on me. It is not particularly a secret. My guess is they also picked you as my negotiating partner because you look like my ex-wife."

Westhoff was caught off guard by his observation and, for a moment, also seemed to be wondering about her being selected for this assignment. "My country has done the research on you, the famous architect. I was asking as a colleague . . . a fellow architect, a possible friend for today. What was wrong with you and your Frau . . .wife?"

"Passion for work instead of passion for life, not her life, I suppose," Titus said. "Say, how far will you go for your country or a friend? You saved my life, our lives, today."

Westhoff said, "I rely on my country for my life and the privilege to have this refuge. Friends can be . . . sometimes . . . more valuable for living."

"What happens if I do not change my mind about the building? Will I end up like Stecker, a victim of politics encased in a block of concrete?"

"Herr Stecker was where he should not have been. I am sorry for that. My country protects itself sometimes, in harsh ways, to enemies and its own people."

"I'm not an enemy. What is your opinion about my current situation?" asked Titus.

"If I do not gain your cooperation, I will have failed, I am afraid—somewhat like Herr Stecker in his responsibility. Possibly, you will also have failed in realizing your building."

"Only a bad compromise is a failure," said Titus, reaching deep into a Howard Roark mental state.

"I am asking you to work with me on this, for me and for you," Westhoff said, intently looking at Titus, eye to eye.

Titus leaned into her look, and she didn't blink. He wondered if she thought he might kiss her. He didn't know himself. He leaned in even closer, shut his eyes, took a deep breath through his nose and released it like a cleansing breath.

Westhoff pulled her head back. "What are you doing?"

"A little research. I am . . . smelling . . . you," he said, a hint of an apology in his tone.

"Was? Warum?" She smelled her sleeves and hands to check what he could be smelling.

Titus knew why he was sniffing but was worried about what her reaction would be to the truth. "There is a certain scent that someone told me was part of being an East German. It is the smell of coal burning and time standing still and perhaps despair mixed with pride. You are very different than what I imagined when they said there would be a comrade architect from the East working on the project."

Westhoff continued to smell her hands and sleeves. "And how do I smell?"

"You smell like all these plants and sunshine, actually—a little like paradise. Not like all the coal-smoke pollution outside in East Germany. One might say that West Berlin is a little fresh air within East Germany, an island in a sea."

"Officially, West Berlin is a sore that will not heal, and there is no East Germany. Only the Deutsche Demokratische Republik, our socialist republic. We are in a worker's paradise, here in the DDR," she said very directly with only a slight mocking tone.

"You do not smell of despair, but maybe of some loneliness, of being in a prison masquerading as a paradise. I sense a certain untapped potential in your life here, like someone who has never tasted the nectar of the gods or the forbidden fruit. For you to leave here, it would be like releasing a bird from a cage that has never used its wing."

"That is how you look at it from your side of the Wall, but I am not trapped as you see it. Who is inside and who is outside? We are here in an enclosed garden," she made a sweeping gesture, "inside East Berlin, outside West Berlin, inside the DDR, outside your Bundesrepublik."

"But we are on the same side of the Wall now, at least your side of the Wall. Your little piece of the wall is a Garden of Eden within East Germany . . . the DDR."

"I am going to change now out of this uniform of my worker's paradise, too much, how you call it, stiff starch," she said. "Maybe I will find some Feigen Blaetter . . . fig leaves to wear."

She stood and moved to a different curtain at the other end of the space, away from the kitchen. He could see it was a sleeping area, as the foot of a bed stuck out in view from the opening of the curtain. Titus watched as the curtain closed in front of the bed and poured another drink for both of them. He then stood up and walked toward the curtain. He stopped as he could see her shadow undressing behind the curtain.

Titus felt 'at home' based on the conversation but then snapped back to the situation at hand. Here he was with a woman who was responsible for getting him to agree to change his design. She also had a pistol in her briefcase.

He walked a bit closer to the curtain slowly, and he noticed that she was looking at him through the curtain.

"Is this an extension of the Iron Curtain?" Titus asked, slightly touching the fabric.

"That depends," came the reply from behind the curtain.

"Have you ever known someone, been with someone from the West?" Titus pressed with a soft voice.

"Like now, with you?"

"Like now, I guess," said Titus, thinking this was not what he had expected to feel in this situation with Westhoff, possibly an opponent for his project. There was an attraction here. He could not deny it. Had she been picked because she looked like his wife, as additional persuasion? Was he finally coming out of his depressed state at this time and in this odd place?

His line of thought was interrupted as she pulled back the curtain divider. Her blond hair was down, and she wore a different white blouse, one that was unbuttoned down at the neck. Her pants had been replaced by cut-off army fatigue pants.

Her military atmosphere had disappeared, and registering Titus's response to her appearance, she said, "I am still human like you, East or West. I just happen to have been in a different place when a political decision was made."

Titus focused on her eyes. "What can you smell on me?"

"I smell the stubbornness you mentioned, and freedom, and a passion for your work, no compromising. I know, even as someone in the East, that freedom can be intoxicating. We cannot see what life is like in West Berlin except from not permitted television, but we can smell it sometimes and hear it when the wind is right."

"That's not really like tasting freedom, is it?"

"No, it isn't." She leaned toward Titus, leading with her nose toward him for his scent, and then closer with her lips to his lips for a hesitant kiss.

He returned the kiss and pulled her to him. He could smell both the flowers of her garden and the odor of the East. The setting sun flowed through her hair as he ran his fingers through it. She returned the embrace and continued to kiss him as if she had gone beyond capturing a scent and was now drinking him in, her passion for him clear as she pulled off his jacket.

Titus ran his hands down her neck and pulled her loose blouse off her back. He stepped her back in his arms, through the curtain, and to the bed. The curtain continued to flow over them as they lowered to the bed. They took turns pulling off each other's clothing, and the warmth of her body made him melt from any stiffness to a molten state. She continued to consume him, as his body softened, with her hair, her lips, and her touches, and she and he entered a different world, far away from political divisions and self-control, as the light streamed into the greenhouse onto the two entwined bodies partially covered by the single sheet of the bed.

THE WALL

Chapter Five

As the sun rose, the light crossed Titus's face, and it woke him. He raised up, looked at the splash of blond hair on the pillow, and bent over to give her a kiss. Her space had a new glow in the morning, beyond the spartan design of the space. As he placed his hand on her bare shoulder, she turned her head into the sunlight, which shone through her blue eyes. She sat up slowly and leaned on him, looking toward the sunlight. They enjoyed the sun streaming in on them, closing their eyes and opening them only to look at each other.

"This all seems like a dream, a surreal one, but I never thought I would end up spending the night sleeping in the shadow of the Wall. Your wall, at least," Titus spoke softly.

"Plenty of time to sleep here, to escape a bit, but we do not have good dreams, I think. I wish I could wake up, and my life here would just be a bad dream, but I know different."

Titus continued on that thought, "Crazy meetings, dead spies, car chases with guns, and this little oasis of paradise. I do not want to wake up." He smiled. "Maybe I will stay."

This triggered an alarmed response from Westhoff, "Your visa! That you had to get to the trailer, crossing the border. Is it for one day or two days?"

"I don't know. I don't think I have a visa, at least not in my passport. I was escorted across, right before the meeting."

"Scheisse!"

"Is that a problem?"

She settled down, biting her lip as she seemed to consider his question. "For you especially, and for me. We must get back, at least to the construction site, without being found out here, outside the city, like this," referring to their present state of undress.

She pulled the bedsheet around her and began to dress in her original outfit. He, too, began to dress. One piece here and another there. After a flurry of finding and handing each their clothes and Westhoff grabbing her briefcase, they headed quickly to the car, looking in the distance for anyone watching them. They drove out through the woods and onto the main road.

Titus and Westhoff drove in silence, eyes focused in front of them. Occasionally, he would glance at her worried expression and then behind them to see if anyone was following.

They passed a black sedan on the side of the road, and as they passed, he heard the car start up and pull out behind them. Titus grabbed her shoulder and pointed backward.

She turned to look, then faced forward and gripped the steering wheel tightly. She accelerated, and the car behind them sped up in measure, with the car behind eventually pulling alongside them on the driver's side.

The driver of the other car was dressed in a military uniform, and the passenger indicated to Westhoff that she should follow them, but she remained looking forward. The car swerved toward her driver's door and then pulled in front of them. With no choice, they stayed behind the other car and followed it, still not speaking to each other.

As they drove, Titus could tell they were approaching the city and heading back to the construction site on the East Berlin side. When they arrived, the men in the other car ushered them to the construction trailer with a certain forceful stride. Titus and Westhoff entered the trailer with their escorts standing behind them. They faced two stern-looking men in drab gray suits, just as Titus might expect from KGB agents in a movie. *Not KGB*, he thought. *What were they called? Stasi, that's it.*

The first man spoke, "Herr Dare, you have overstayed your welcome, perhaps. You were approved to only visit the factory and return. Where were you?"

Westhoff began to speak, but Titus cut her off. "At the factory looking at concrete."

"All night?" the man challenged.

"We had car trouble," Titus said, hoping for a quick resolution to the interrogation.

"Herr Dare, I have a daughter who uses the same excuse when she is out past curfew with her boyfriend. I was expecting something more creative out of you," the man said, smiling but then frowning. "There was an accident at the factory with one of the building pieces, and we need to question Fraulein Westhoff about it. Fraulein, you will assist us in this, verstehen?"

"She had nothing to do with . . . him . . . any accident at the factory," Titus broke in.

"With him? Him, you say? What does that mean?" The man gave Titus a hard look.

Titus stumbled with his thoughts and, subsequently, with his words. "With him . . . I assumed the, uh, a person involved with the accident was a worker there."

"I did not mention anyone or an injury," the man said. One of the building blocks was broken open at the factory, and Fraulein Westhoff will assist us in working through this so there will be no delay for the project and the foundation-stone ceremony."

Titus stayed with his line of defense. "She was not involved."

"I did not say she was involved. I said she must help us."

As Titus looked at Westhoff, she motioned with a slight

shake of her head for Titus to be quiet.

The second man, seeming impatient, said, "She is responsible for the project," and he moved toward them and took her arm firmly.

"Let go of her." Titus moved to stop him. "I demand that you release her."

The first man spoke up, "You are not in a position to demand anything. We will give a report to Herr Schmidt, and he will contact you about this incident."

Titus would not allow this, and he continued his opposition, trying to remove the man's hand from Westhoff's arm. "Let go of her. . ."

The second man then grabbed Titus's arm, bending it behind his back, and pushed Titus toward the door. Titus struggled against the uncomfortable hold, but still, out the door, he went. He was then escorted to the edge of the Wall, and the armed guard at the checkpoint gate pushed Titus through the checkpoint.

Titus walked away, reluctant, and after a moment of reflection, he turned to head back through the checkpoint again. He could see Westhoff being escorted by two men into a black limousine car, or at least the East German version of a limousine. As Titus started walking back to the checkpoint at the Wall, the armed guard from the East at the checkpoint, who held a machine gun, blocked his way into the checkpoint.

Chapter Six

Titus started walking away from the Wall and then turned to face it, staring at it up and down as if he were sizing it up. He walked back up to the Wall and then along the Wall, along its length, pressing his hand against it. He picked up his pace until he was running beside the Wall as if to find an endpoint to get around it.

He ran past a bicycle that was leaning up against the Wall. To the side of the bicycle, there was a very distinctive graffiti mural—an illusion that the Wall was being opened up to a background of plants and animals, like a lush garden. He stared at the image of the garden, thinking about Westhoff and the previous night. He tried to look through the mural and to the future. He glanced back at the bicycle he had passed, walked to it, pulled the bicycle under him, and started to ride, first wobbly and then determinedly. He kept pedaling beside the wall and then along streets where the path next to the wall was interrupted, over cobblestones, gravel, and dirt, achieving a certain forward drive of motion on the bicycle.

He continued to glance at the Wall to his side while still focused on the way forward, always looking for a way in through the Wall. As his path veered toward the Wall, he would kick it every so often and then regain his balance after the kick. His face mirrored his anger, and his feet on the pedals showed his hatred for the Wall as he rode. This anger kept him going, pedaling as a way of fighting against the Wall. He continued down the streets, along canals, through forests, working his way around the entire inside perimeter of the Wall, trapped inside West Berlin but feeling as if he were on the outside trying to get in. His anger energy was now absorbed by the pedaling of the bicycle, but a certain calmness began to fill Titus.

As he continued to leave the urban area of West Berlin, the Wall was also transforming itself, from the sophisticated, threatening urban barrier structure to the more primitive but still effective fence out in the suburban area of Berlin. The sun began to set, but Titus rode deep into the evening and into forest paths at the farthest point from the center of Berlin. Out here, the Wall was sometimes close and sometimes far away. Titus constantly searched it out, looking for the lights along the Wall.

His emotional tone changed from his earlier anger to one of quiet resolution and almost to some sort of tenderness toward the Wall. He kept pedaling, now nearly in a trance with his trajectory, no longer looking for a way through the Wall but seeing it as a fellow traveler in his journey to understanding what was happening to him. His focus began to dissolve as the rural surroundings turned back to streets and buildings. He began to slow down, and he looked around as the street scene began to look familiar to him.

By now, it was very early in the morning, still dark but

becoming light, when he realized he had passed the construction job site where he had started, where he had been pushed outside the Wall. He looked around in a circle, realizing in a disoriented way that he was indeed right back where he had started. He pedaled the bicycle back to where he found it, with the same graffiti mural next to it. It sank in that he had ridden all the way around Berlin, West Berlin that is, but along the inside of the Berlin Wall.

Titus muttered to himself, "Back where I started. That figures for my life. Me trapped on the outside, of East Berlin, or inside West Berlin, wanting to get in from where everyone wants to escape to."

He got off the bicycle, and his knees buckled a bit from the ride. It was then he realized he had ridden all night around the inside perimeter of West Berlin.

Addressing the Wall out loud now, he said, "What is it with you? You bring me back here, you let me in, and then you put me out. No wonder you are a 'she' instead of an 'it,' all makes sense."

Just then, a matronly Berliner woman surprised him by walking behind him and giving him a prickly look. He thought she may have understood his comment on gender. Instead, she took hold of the bicycle's handlebars and walked it away with one last disapproving look at Titus.

As Titus watched her disappear along the Wall, he noticed

there was a light on in a construction trailer on the west side of the Wall, next to the one he had first entered the day before. The trailer had a sign on the door: *Schlesinger TiefBau.*

He walked over to the trailer, curious about the light being on so early in the morning. He climbed up the trailer's stairs and slowly opened the door... and saw someone, with his back to him, looking at a set of drawings at the table.

Titus said, "Hello," but the person did not respond, and he could now tell from the full head of hair, it was the excavator from the meeting the day before, so Titus approached him quietly to not startle him. At the table, he could see over the man's shoulder. It was a foundation plan that he recognized as his building and another drawing, an old parchment drawing, that was stamped with an eagle over a swastika in the corner of the drawing. The man, now sensing Titus's presence, rolled up the parchment plan from the table and turned to face him.

Titus spoke first, "I recognize you. You're the excavator I met in the trailer yesterday."

The man responded, "And you are the architect who likes his building the way it is and will not compromise."

"Would you?" Titus challenged.

"If it were better. I just follow orders and dig holes where I am told, usually as the drawings show."

"What was that drawing you were looking at? It looked very historical. Is that from our site?"

"Just the building plans, to see how different my work will be when they turn your building," clarified the excavator.

"I meant the older drawing, and how are you confident that my building will get turned?"

"Na ja, I can tell these things. I have worked in Berlin, and under Berlin, for a long time. As you can imagine, I am as surprised as you, especially since I am the first one under the ground."

"Do you know why they are turning it beyond the rather weak political excuse they gave?" Titus asked, feeling like he might actually get an honest answer.

"Here in Berlin, you can trust that you cannot trust anything to be as it is . . . or anybody. Split personalities in a divided ciyt, courtesy of the end of the war."

"So, what is in the ground under the building now? And if it gets turned, what is there in the ground then? And . . . what is that other drawing you had?"

"They are just the drawings, your drawings," stated the excavator firmly.

"No, I meant that other roll in your hand," Titus asked,

pointing at the parchment the man was holding.

"It is just an old survey, nichts zu sehen. It is nothing."

"May I see it?"

The man reluctantly set the rolled drawing on the table. "It is not that interesting."

"Old surveys are fascinating, to me. That looks like it's drawn on parchment, so it must be about fifty years old. Am I right?"

"As I say, it is nothing of interest. Just shows where some things are that will need to be worked around."

Titus nodded his head toward the drawing, and the excavator begrudgingly unrolled it. Titus moved closer to the table, bending over it to look at the plan.

"Hmm, this is from 1938. Look at the exquisite drafting and ink line work..." He paused, then "Is that a swastika in the corner? Is this a plan for the same area as my building? That looks like where the Wall would be."

"Ja, das stimmt. You have it correct," confirmed the excavator pointing at the drawing.

"What kind of structure is that here? On the east side of the Wall, a building footprint," Titus said, pointing at a specific area on the drawings. "The walls are massive."

"It is an old bunker, concrete, from before the war, but for the war."

"What a nightmare for you to remove. Is it still there? It didn't show up on the surveys given to us for the design competition if I remember correctly."

"Na ja, the bunkers from the war were a little secret, still a secret," mused the man.

"So, if this is the street here, where my building is, my building would miss the bunker completely as originally planned. If they turn it, they will have to dig down around the bunker on the east side."

"Stimmt. That is true."

Titus was dumbfounded. "Well, that seems like a good reason *not* to turn it."

"One would think, but one does not know about these things," mused the excavator.

"So, the Wall currently runs down the middle of an old street, according to this. No building foundations in the street. What is this on your old drawing that would be running right under the Wall?" Titus studied the drawing closely.

"It is an old tunnel connecting to the bunker, labeled as a sewer to conceal its function."

"So, how do you have these drawings? Do only you have these drawings?"

"I have been under the ground many times here in Berlin, and I have to find these things out. Underground surprises are never good for construction, and Berlin has many buried, how you might say, bodies, sometimes harmless, sometimes dangerous, like one of your bombs from above. Berlin underground is a Friedhof, you call them graveyards I believe, our word is literally peace-yard. Except, as I said, bombs and not bodies."

"So where did you get it, the map?" enquired Titus.

"They are from an archive from the original engineer for the bunker," replied the excavator, letting the drawing roll back up.

"Ahh, the name here on the drawing is *Schlesinger*." Titus paused. "That is your last name, yes? Is this your father?"

"Ja, stimmt. Yes, correct. An architect and a detective, I see."

"That is quite a coincidence that you are working back on the same site."

The man smirked. "Yes, is it not?"

"Is your father still alive?"

"He is, but he is in the East with the rest of my family. Die Mauer, sorry, the Wall divides my life and my heart, you see. I wish I could blink, and it would go away. Diese verdammte Wall muss weg. It must go away."

Titus guessed at his last statement. "You and me both. That line of vertical concrete wall has completely changed my design and made a mess of my life here in just one day. But..."

"But. . . it has not separated you from your family for the last forty years," countered the excavator.

"How did you end up in the West?" Titus asked.

"I am an excavator, makes movement from place to place easy, sometimes. Not easy for my family, as it turned out."

Titus smiled, understanding the implication of the man's statement about excavating and the underground. "My work, in particular, separated me from my wife," he said, talking more to himself than to the man, "and now this project from someone else important."

"Ahh, Fraulein Westhoff. She likes you, I could tell," observed the excavator.

Titus was surprised and embarrassed initially at this observation, but he swept the feelings aside. "Maybe not after today. I'm afraid I have gotten her into some bad trouble. And I'm not sure whose side she is on, maybe on both sides."

"Right now, she is on the east side of the Wall with the so-called Todesstreifen—death strip—making the thinness of the Wall quite wide, and quite dangerous."

"The death strip?" Titus asked.

"The area along the Wall, on the east side. Trouble comes to those who try to reach the Wall from the East . . . and also to those who do not compromise with the Wall," the excavator said with a sly grin aimed directly at Titus.

Titus was intrigued. "So, do you think the bunker is important to this project?"

"It could be nothing; it could be something. It could be the lost wealth of a madman or one of his follies. It is in the way; that is for sure."

To himself, Titus thought, *Ghosts and buried treasure, what else should I expect?* And then, speaking to the excavator, "Do you think the Wall will ever come down? That would solve my problem and yours . . . but probably not soon enough, especially for me."

The excavator thought about it. "I have this dream that, like the walls of Jericho in the Bible, we will march along the Wall one day and make a big noise, and it will fall down. Then this nonsense in Berlin will make sense. I am not sure the East and West are ready now to face each other without the Eiserner Vorhang, the Iron Curtain."

"That is an interesting thought, from the Bible, but wishful thinking, I am afraid," replied Titus.

"Ja, das stimmt. I must go. I have much to do," said the excavator, pulling the drawings into a single pile.

"I am not sure what I am going to do," Titus remarked.

"You have a building to save . . . and now a fellow architect to save."

"I wish I had your view of it."

"My view is from below. Tomorrow is another day on both sides of the Wall. You must pick your sides and your choice wisely."

The excavator rolled up the old parchment drawing last, gave a small salute with the drawing to Titus, and left the construction trailer. Titus looked down at the remaining drawings of his building. He shook his head and then hit the drawing on the table with his clenched fist.

He left the trailer and started walking back to his hotel, or at least in the direction where he thought his hotel was. As he walked, a car, a Trabant, pulled up behind him at a distance and turned on its headlights. He whirled around to face the car and gave it a hard look. The car backed off and veered away from him. He nodded at the car and went back to walking.

After a few wrong turns, it became full morning as Titus made it back to the hotel. He was walking very slowly from being tired, sore from the bike ride and the state of things. He returned the greeting of the hotel clerk with a faint wave and headed to the elevator and then down the hotel corridor.

Upon entering his room, Titus looked around for any uninvited visitors. Seeing none, he sat on the bed and thought about the day before, the night, his life, his ex-wife, and Westhoff. He was too tired to think about his options, the risks, and what would make this situation resemble some of his previous life when it had been somewhat normal.

Looking at his watch, he realized he had not slept a wink. He looked at himself in the mirror over the dresser and decided that what he saw was worse than how he felt. He went into the bathroom, took another look at his face, shook his head, pulled his shirt off, and splashed water on his face. After roughly drying his face, he returned to the bedroom with the towel still in his hand, rubbing his neck and face.

He was startled by what he saw before him—a man sitting in the lounge chair in his room, next to the window in the shadows. He was dressed in plain dark non-descript suit that almost blended into the armchair he was sitting in.

"Long day . . . and night?" asked the man.

"Who are you? Doesn't anyone knock on the door in this hotel?" Titus scoffed.

"You look like hell."

"Well, it was not my usual day. I had my design completely changed and found a dead body. I've been shot at, involved in a car chase, threatened, and then thrown out of East Berlin and away from my project, which is the only reason I am in Berlin in the first place. And now you pop up in my hotel room."

"I work with Stecker. Potter is my name."

"You mean *worked*," corrected Titus, testing to see if Potter would catch the nuance.

Potter leaned in, resting his elbows on his knees. "What do you mean by that, exactly?"

"We saw him, in concrete, dead. The foundation-stone for my building has become his tombstone."

"What?! Are you sure? What happened?" Potter became agitated, now dropping his cool demeanor and jumping up out of the chair he was in. He rotated once to the window and then faced Titus again. "Dammit all . . . Tell me everything."

"We, uh, the German girl. Frieda, Fraulein Westhoff . . ."

"The woman architect, you mean."

"Yes, she is the architect from the East. She and I, well, we went to the concrete factory and were looking at the structural beams and then saw the foundation-stone, which turned out to be Stecker or at least Stecker's hand pushed inside of it and covered with concrete. We were then chased out of there by some soldiers, shot at, and escaped in a car. In my mind, the foundation-stone already has an epitaph on it, *mine*, as far as I can tell, in terms of working on this project," Titus said, trying to find some humor, though admittedly dark, in the situation.

"How could you tell it was Stecker?" Potter asked, his mouth still hanging open in disbelief.

"Same watch as you're wearing," Titus said, pointing at Potter's wrist. "Have heard from him?"

"No, dammit all. If that was him, this is terrible. The Cold War is supposed to be cold, not evil," Potter said, running fingers through his hair and regaining his composure. "What about the overnight with the girl? What is her role in all this?"

"How do you know about that, where I was? And I don't know what to think about Fraulein Westhoff, except she is also a victim in this, I think."

"They told me about your little adventure . . . indirectly. We bug them; the East bugs us. They made no mention of Stecker. This is worse than we had expected, but it explains why we have not heard from him."

"Maybe that explains the wires in Stecker's hand, in the

concrete," Titus offered.

"That is what Stecker was investigating. We think they were putting listening devices and worse in the concrete beams, since they control the building construction in that factory."

"Who are *they*?" asked Titus.

"The East, the secret police, our counterparts, and their outside operatives and beyond, those behind the project."

"And whose side are you, *we*, on with all of this?"

"My side, our side, your side. I am going to need your help."

"So, help? My help has not been helpful. What do you want from me?"

"What is the girl's involvement?" Potter pressed.

"She is an architect, picked for this project to get me to compromise on the design, by her own admission. She handles herself pretty well in car chases and dodging the police. She does have a file on me and a gun."

"This is the Cold War, everybody has a file on everybody else, and if she was not given the gun, she probably found it. Remember, we are at ground zero here for post-World War II. I'm not sure whose side she's really on, but probably her own if there is a chance to get to the West. Anything else that seems important in this that is keeping you and me alive?"

"That's it," Titus said after a pause. "I think she is stuck in the middle of this mess, like me, but she cannot cross over."

"So, where did you stay last night?"

"She has a summer cottage retreat of sorts," Titus responded evasively, with little confidence in his dodging the question.

"Yes, we know. I was just checking to see if you're going to play it straight with us. Never know who is who, or who is telling the truth."

Titus grimaced. "I know who I am. Not sure about anyone else, including you."

"So, nothing like sleeping with the enemy," Potter said with a smirk. "West meets East, a little détente, some negotiations, and a break in the Cold War."

"That is none of your business."

"Maybe, but stuff like that has turned some of our best agents. Remember what my business is. This, *she*, is what will keep you out of trouble or out of a concrete block."

"She seems to waver between dedication to East Germany and a wish for a different life," Titus offered.

"Hmm, profile sounds like she has been enlisted by the secret police to work on you, maybe willingly, maybe not, as this is a chance to get closer to the West, for them and for her. They probably have some control over her, some blackmail of a family member, perhaps. The soldiers chasing you probably didn't know who she was or who she was working for."

"Well, she lost them with some evasive driving, some funny driver's education they have in East Germany," Titus said.

"Or they're managing appearances, whoever was chasing you when they found out who she was with," offered Potter.

"So, how do I fit in? They have already decided to turn my building ninety degrees, and the foundation-stone is ready to go. She thinks there is some other reason for the building being turned—unofficially, that is."

Potter said, "We need you to stay close to her. Probably not a problem, apparently, after last night. From what we hear, she is in a bit of trouble. She was probably supposed to just keep you entertained, for creating an open mind, not to keep you alive as well. We need to get you back on the inside of this thing."

"I am just a bloody architect with an ego and my own problems, not a secret agent."

"So far, you have been learning pretty quickly. James Bond in one day and a night," remarked Potter with a slight smile again.

"Find another Double-O. I only have a license to design buildings, not to kill."

"You have two things to think about. Your building and the

girl. Both are in trouble and one you made worse with your sleepover."

"I don't think I'm welcome at the moment."

"Maybe, maybe not. We received a message that the building owner from the East would like to meet with you personally, late this afternoon. Which is why I'm here. They would still like to make sure you're part of the foundation-laying ceremony despite your little adventure last night."

"What? Why in the hell is that offer coming now?" Titus exclaimed. "I didn't think forgiveness was such a strong trait among Cain and Abel."

"Cain and Abel?"

"I understand the owners are twins."

"See, you're a natural at this, this intelligence-gathering. Despite the politics, there is a sense that your integrity and participation are key to the building, whichever way it is turned. Some face-saving also in play, perhaps," Potter said.

"My integrity or the building? Seems like everyone has been trying to undo both."

"Well, so far, you're still alive, managed a little honeymoon in the East, and have been invited back for a command performance."

Titus ignored the jabs. "Did you know that the changing of the building puts it right on top of an old World War II bunker, one of Hitler's?"

"How's that? A bunker?" asked Potter, his interest apparently piqued.

"There's a bunker underneath where the east part of the building will be, if it were to be rotated."

"Interesting. I am going to suggest to Herr Johann that you walk that part of the construction site after the meeting with the building owner. See if you can figure out why it is so important to rotate the building."

"They said the turning of the building has to do with not opening up the Wall, too soon for the politics," Titus explained. "A bunker foundation in the way is an additional wrinkle. Anyway, it is your job to do the spying."

"Technically, yes, but you're in the position of finding out why because you have some skin in this . . . your building, that is."

"Do you know what happened to Westhoff?"

"You may be able to find out when you meet with them."

"So, what's the purpose of this meeting?" Titus asked.

"They still need your blessing, involvement, for some reason, whether good or bad."

"And so, what do I do now?"

"You have a meeting later today, so you had better freshen

up. You look like hell.

"And if I don't go along with this?"

"You won't have a chance to fix your building problem, or at least find out why it is being turned . . . and you won't see your female friend again. She probably won't get her job back, or life back, because of your little excursion. That was probably not part of her assignment. Or maybe she volunteered herself for a more unintentionally dangerous assignment. You might be able to somehow fix that, at least."

"I'm not sure whose side I'm on in this anymore, or she is. Whose side are you on again?" Titus asked.

"Right now, I'm on your side, *and* my side."

"How can I tell who is on which side?" Titus pressed.

"You can't, at least not in Berlin. Everybody can be on both sides or just one side. That's the problem with a city with a wall down the middle," Potter said. "I like your building, if that's any consolation."

Potter started to leave but turned back to face Titus. "You're expected at the construction trailer at 6:00 p.m. Oh, by the way, I wouldn't mention the concrete bunker thing to anyone. Any Hitler stuff makes everyone a little jumpy here. If true, you may be onto something that isn't good for your building . . . or your health . . . or me, based on what they did to Stecker."

Titus nodded, then remembered something. "Wait. You should know … I think the excavator on the construction site has some plans showing a tunnel under the Wall as well, to the bunker."

Potter gave him a puzzled look. "Somehow, it doesn't surprise me. See? You're a natural in the spy business."

Potter again turned to leave and gave Titus a slight wave over his shoulder.

Titus watched as the door closed. He walked to the door to lock it and then moved to the window to look outside, up and down the street. A Trabant idled in a plume of smoke in front of the hotel, and he shook his head, turned into the room, and started to undress, heading into the bathroom. He turned on the shower and closed his eyes, hoping the warm water would wash his stress away.

After the shower, he got dressed and lay down on the bed, fully clothed, with his eyes shut. It was late afternoon, and he found some solace in his rest until the hotel room phone rang. The female voice on the phone indicated it was his pre-arranged phone call for a wakeup call. Surprised, as he had not ordered a wakeup call, Titus thanked the receptionist and shook his head at the state of things.

He left the hotel, waving for a taxicab. As he opened the car door, a familiar voice greeted him from previous taxi rides.

"Well, hallo again. How did you find the Wall? Gut?"

"More than I could ever imagine," replied Titus.

"Gut, another happy tourist. So, where to this time?"

"Mauerstrasse and Friedrichstrasse again," Titus managed the pronunciation fairly well. "Same as the last ride, you remember.

"Natuerlich and your German is getting much better."

The taxicab arrived at the construction trailer on the west side of the Wall, and Titus entered the trailer to find Potter was already there, waiting to greet him.

"Well, you look a little better now. They're waiting for you at the construction trailer on the other side. My understanding is they're willing to give you one more chance at cooperation."

"What about Frieda, Fraulein Westhoff?" asked Titus.

"Well, I would say that it is up to you to negotiate, maybe your bargaining chip, if she means that much to you to compromise. The foundation-stone ceremony is still scheduled for tomorrow, so you're going to have to think quickly."

"Can't you and your spooks do something?"

"We cannot chance turning the Cold War into a hot one. In one night, you managed to heat things up. We will have someone watching in on you, but they'll be undercover, can't really surface."

"Do you know where she is?"

"Westhoff? She's *around*, according to Johann. Under close watch, but she knows the most about the project and is also their hold on you, apparently. The best we, you, can hope for is to smooth things over and play ball with them."

"Maybe I should just leave Berlin."

"Not good for us, for her, and remember, you're in the middle of East Germany on a little island of West Berlin, where there is some freedom to not compromise. Lucky for you. Let's go."

Titus and Potter headed through the checkpoint in the Wall and entered the construction trailer on the east side. Herr Schmidt and Herr Johann were there with some other serious East German authority-looking types.

Herr Schmidt, the East German project manager, spoke first, "Herr Dare, it is good to see you back. We hope you had a successful, perhaps unusual, visit yesterday."

"What do you want from me?" replied Titus brusquely.

Potter gave Titus a warning look and whispered, "Easy there."

Ignoring Titus's question, Herr Schmidt continued, "As before, your skills as an architect are required, as a creative negotiator, someone who knows how to build a bridge across problems."

Titus broke back in, "Where is Fraulein Westhoff?"

Herr Schmidt, again ignoring the question but now focusing on Titus, said, "The builders of the project would like to meet with you in person, at a villa outside the city. If you would, please," and he motioned toward the door of the trailer.

Titus glanced at Potter with a worried look, and Potter shrugged. The entire group exited the trailer, and outside, Titus was motioned by two darkly dressed men toward an East German-model limousine. He stepped into the car with a last look to Potter and then was driven off. All Potter could do was wave and shake his head.

The limousine gradually left the city, headed past large, rather grim housing blocks, and entered a more wooded area with villas, some in good shape and some still suffering from World War II. The limousine arrived at a severe but renovated classical-looking villa, and Titus was shown in through the front door. He stepped into a heavily wood-paneled room off the entry. The door was shut behind him. As he looked around, he saw the room had samples on all the walls of barbed wire, framed, and displayed, with labels on them in German and English. KOREA, POLAND, CZECHOSLOVAKIA, GERMANY, YUGOSLAVIA, ALBANIA, CUBA, CAMBODIA, USSR, CHINA, VIETNAM, and other countries. His gaze around the room was interrupted by a sound behind him.

A man dressed somewhere between a butler and bodyguard

said to Titus, "Herr Zwillinge will see you now."

Titus was escorted by the man into a large, imperial-looking office with a high, ornate ceiling and floor-to-ceiling windows. The escort turned, went back into the hall, and closed the door behind him. Titus walked up to a large, executive, wood-carved desk, where a large man turned around in the chair that was facing away from Titus. Titus recognized the man as his companion from the train compartment on the way to Berlin, but he did not know how to actually respond, based on all that had happened since the train ride.

"You . . . you were on the train with me," said Titus, focusing on the man.

The man looked puzzled. "Bitte?"

Titus continued, "You were the man on the train from Frankfurt to Berlin. In my train compartment."

"You must be thinking of someone else," responded the man with a very faint grin.

"I don't know. Well, he could be your twin."

"And so I am," said a different man stepping in from a door to an adjoining room.

The first man said to Titus, "You must have ridden with my brother here," gesturing to the second man.

"So who are you?" Titus looked at the first man and then the second man. "And you?"

The man in the chair said, "We are the builders of your building. I am Assa, and this is my brother Jakob."

"You two are the developers of Berlin Tor?"

Assa affirmed, "Ja, that is us."

"But I thought it was a joint construction project between the East and West."

"It is. We just happen to be related. It makes it easier," Jakob followed up.

"Which of you is which? Which side are each of you from?" probed Titus. He could only see a slight difference in their appearance, in their faces, with only their suits being distinctive in tailoring, one showing more refinement.

"Both and none. It does not really matter . . . I am from the West," said Jakob.

Titus retorted, "It matters to me, and to the design of a project that straddles two worlds."

Jakob continued, "That is what makes this project so interesting to us and to you, apparently."

"So why am I here? Now?"

"First, a little historical Hintergrund, er, background. The

Wall has special significance for us," said Jakob.

Assa joined in, "You see, we, our family, earlier in our lives, lived near where the Wall was built. We were playing, how you say, hide-and-seek, near the border of the Russian sector and American sector on the day in August when the Wall went up. I was on one side, and he," pointing to Jakob, "was on the other. But as you see, we have overcome that difficulty."

"So how did you get all this," Titus gestured around the room, "and what is the room with all the barbed wire?"

Assa began, "It is a bittersweet thing. The barbed wire is both the source of our separation and power. Our father's construction company provided all the barbed wire and then the concrete for the Wall to the East German authorities and then for all the fences and walls throughout the world where Communist ideals prevailed. It is a captive market, one might say." He smiled at his pun for a moment and then became more serious. "Our father, however, did not know that my brother and I would be on different sides of the Wall when he delivered the materials for the Wall, and up it went where we were. Even he, with all his connections to the authorities, could not bring us together. However, my brother and I now benefit from his freedom," pointing at his brother Jacob, "and my staying behind here in the East."

"So, you are the builders of my building at the Wall, built on money made from building walls that separate people."

"Ja, that seems so," said Jakob as Assa nodded, saying, "And you are the designer, and that is why you are valuable to us."

"Where is Fraulein Westhoff?" asked Titus in a demanding tone, becoming frustrated at what was adding an extra layer of absurdity to his life.

Assa continued, "She has been removed from the project as a security measure for her safety. Her time is over. She is no longer valuable for your cooperation. We thought she would be able to persuade you to cooperate, but she has apparently not lived up to the task of convincing you."

"Persuade me with what?"

"With her understanding and companionship. Your visit with her was pleasant, was it not?" answered Assa.

"Are you saying that was her job? To seduce me? Like some business trade for her work on me. I can't believe that," replied Titus, looking from one twin to the other.

Jacob added, "You should be sensitive to the value of that. You act like you do not compromise, but you have already. As long as there is a need for you to find work, you are no different."

"Fraulein Westhoff, what will happen to her?" pressed Titus.

Assa adjusted himself in his chair and put his fingers in a

triangle on the desk, "Well, let us see if we can work out a compromise with someone who apparently does not compromise."

Resembling one part of a wrestling tag team now, Jakob said, "Let me ask you a question . . . How would you answer the following question? What is your favorite project?"

Titus had an answer ready from many past job interviews for work. "The next one, of course. Every designer looks forward to the next problem challenge."

And Assa added quickly, "Exactly as we expected. So come with us."

The twins and Titus, following a hand gesture by the twins in unison, walked to two cloth-covered tables. They pulled off the cover of one of them. The table had what appeared to be an architectural model on it.

"Where is that?" asked Titus as he gazed upon the uncovered model that resembled a section of city.

Looking full of pride, Assa said, "That is the new Berlin when the Wall is gone. There will be lots of development when things change."

"So you profit from the splitting of the city and then the reunification? How do you know when the Wall will come down to even think about planning this?"

Jakob began to explain, "Beneath all politics is survival and each person's chance at a little paradise—worker's paradise or free market. We have learned to survive either way."

Titus, trying to grasp all this but thinking strategically about the future, said, "So, you want to buy my cooperation on the Berlin Tor by this future work? Patronage is a bit out of date, but it seems like bribery is still alive."

Assa calmly replied, "You make it sound like we are buying your soul. We are just offering you a creative future."

"We would like to offer you a leading role in the rebuilding of a reunified Berlin and a special attraction. It would keep you very busy and out of trouble," added Jakob as he uncovered the second model.

Titus looked at the two architectural models in front of him. The first one looked like a normal urban development, with the small surprise of recognizing his own building as part of the development. The other model looked like a gray mix between an amusement park and a concentration camp. "So, what is that there, Phase 2?" he asked, pointing to the now uncovered second model.

"That is a special project," said Assa.

"It looks like an East Berlin Disneyland, the grim part of the Magical Kingdom."

Assa continued, "It is a part of Berlin, but a special place, or should I say a special time. It is, how you say, a theme park."

"An amusement park?" asked Titus incredulously.

Assa continued with a certain pride, "No, there will be no amusement. It is more of a model city of how life was, is. We know the Wall will not last forever, but our wager with the future is that there will always be nostalgia for it. West Germans, who have never been, will come to see how it is, and East Germans will want to visit it to remember how it was."

He paused to see Titus's reaction. "So, you see, we need the Wall to stay up for a few more years for the planning of the one project and then some time for the nostalgia to sink in. That is where we need your cooperation. Your building is too risky, too open too soon. It opens a connection hole too soon. The building needs to change the way we have suggested, to keep the Wall closed, no gates, just a bridge from side to side controlled by us."

"And you are banking . . . betting on the timing of the Wall coming down with one project and then banking on a certain nostalgia for the old misery behind the Wall."

Assa registered his understanding and slight discomfort, "That sounds very negative, but much of our future depends on your building and your cooperation."

"That is giving my building and me, a lot of credit to risk

gambling on a change in the future. Seems like there is a deeper problem that you have to make this rather silly effort to turn the building."

Jacob interjected, "Turning the building is a current necessity, better said, not negotiable."

"Is there not some other reason for turning it? Just seems like a whim, despite the reasons you give and the future promises you are making," Titus pressed.

Jacob continued, "As you were told, the Wall removal at the project site creates issues for us. Your building introduces another level of risk with the Wall having a hole, whether real or ceremonial."

"Are you sure there are not some other reasons you need to change the building, move it? Something more, er, fundamental? I understand there are some foundations in the way if you turn the building," Titus said, fishing for some insight on the desired change.

Jacob raised his eyebrows. "Fundamental? That is an interesting choice of words, especially for the German translation. Do you really think there is something under the building?"

"Just . . . it would seem to be a strange, but not unusual, thing to turn the building, to avoid something in the way of the existing foundations, but it seems like you're turning it *toward* a problem," Titus said.

Assa took his turn with reasoning with Titus. "You seem to think you know something about what lies below, or that you think you know something that we have up here," pointing to the side of his forehead and continuing, "Berlin has many things under its soil, but we will deal with it. Turning it is the only way your building will be built at all. Better for us and for you to be built *with* you than without you."

"I'm sure there are lots of things in the ground in an old city like Berlin. Surely, you have to dig around old foundations and cellars . . . bombs and bomb shelters?" Titus probed even further.

Assa countered, "That is always a problem in Berlin, and some look for hidden treasure in the ground from our past history, but like all tomb raiders, usually things turn out badly—for them, at least. Many have dug under our history to find something, but there are lots of dangerous things under our city."

"Such as?" asked Titus.

Becoming impatient, Jacob stressed, "Unexploded bombs, among others, as you noted. One needs to be careful when one digs into areas that they should not. For any treasure below, there are many hazards. But that is in the past. We are here to discuss the proposition in front of us, a larger one than a mere building, your future professionally, and perhaps your, how you say, livelihood."

"My reputation," Titus started," is at stake, which defines my future. Do you mean my livelihood . . . or life?"

Jacob answered, "Your choice on both," and then continued, "You will not have a future unless you claim some minor victories, compromises, here and now. You are indispensable in one sense for the project, but I would not push that too far."

"Do you have some, what is the term, Doppelganger, some Titus Dare lookalike to replace me? A spy trick?" Titus now becoming agitated.

Jacob stated bluntly, "You have read too many spy novels, perhaps. Disposal is far easier than replacement."

"I will only cooperate if Fraulein Westhoff . . . if I can talk to her in private."

"That is not possible. You need to think over our proposition of cooperating and your future. It is not really an offer. It is how things will be. Better with your cooperation, but not impossible without it. A little compromise never hurts; stubbornness, however, can be fatal."

Titus, now with emphasis and belligerence, said, "Only if I can talk to Fraulein Westhoff and she is given her position back. Then I will talk about the future."

Assa was intrigued. "So she means something to you, enough to compromise, I hope. Interessant, and unexpected from such a supposedly focused person on his career, even beyond his past personal relationships."

"I feel responsible for her predicament. It is a condition of my participation, full participation, for her to be free."

Jacob was intrigued. "Free? That is a curious term here in East Berlin. Free in what sense?"

"Back working on the project," Titus clarified.

"So, you have indeed learned from your own past. A woman's value as a companion as compared to a building. I am glad that you are able to compromise for a good reason." Jacob paused to look at Titus more intently.

"We will see you at the foundation-stone laying ceremony, then. Fraulein Westhoff will be there. We will escort you to West Berlin now. You need to be fresh for tomorrow and the future."

"I need to see her first," demanded Titus.

Assa responded, "That is not possible. We have had enough patience with you."

Jacob held up his finger. "Warte mal. I suppose I have a soft spot for architects, maybe for you, in particular," he said, gesturing to the guard. "Lucky for you, she is with us here, safe."

Jacob went to the room door, opened it, and gestured to the guard. Titus was ushered out of the room by the guard and down a long hallway of closed doors in the villa. Titus was stopped at the door and then was motioned in by the guard, who opened the door. Fraulein Westhoff was standing in the room, looking out the window.

She turned at the sound of the door opening and looked at Titus. "You are okay?"

"I wanted to see you, to make sure you are all right . . . but I am not sure about this situation, you and the twins out there."

"Was, why not?" asked Westhoff.

"You seem to have been working for our twin friends out there," said Titus with some coolness in tone.

"How do you mean?" she asked.

Titus continued, "You were to get me to compromise, whatever it took, including the other night."

"Did they tell you that?" asked Westhoff, and then after a pause, "They can think what they want about me, us together, but I did what we did because I felt, for once in my life, alive with a love from outside. No other reason."

"How can I trust you?" Titus moved closer to Westhoff.

Westhoff responded to his approach with outreached arms, "How can you not? Why would I risk telling the truth here, where they could be listening. What I did was what I felt, which is rare in my world, this world." She continued after a concerned pause, "But if you are in here, with me, then you must have made some deal with them, some compromise."

"Not yet. I just wanted to see you, to tell you I am sorry," Titus said.

Westhoff moved a step closer. "You will not compromise, you cannot. I know that only they do not know that."

"I have to do something to get you out of this. I promise I will get you out of this," Titus affirmed with encouragement for Westhoff and himself.

"It is not worth it, a compromise for me. Better for you to save yourself in this," she pressed.

Titus, trying to show further strength as he could see Westhoff was losing any resolve, said, "It is my choice, and I have learned something from you—that I felt more alive in your world than in my world of Titus Dare, the great architect."

"If you compromise, I will not forgive you."

Moving closer, Titus countered, "If I do not, at least for this one time, I will have lost you, as of now."

Titus reached for Westhoff, pulled her close, and embraced her, adding a long, passionate kiss, which was interrupted as the door opened. The guard entered, noted the embrace with disapproval, and motioned in a threatening manner for Titus to leave the room.

Titus was escorted out of the room as Westhoff moved toward the door to leave as well. The guard motioned her back, pulled the door shut, and led Titus down the hallway to the room where the twins were still seated in two chairs, appearing like thrones of judgment to Titus.

Titus confronted them with, "I will see you at the ceremony tomorrow, and Fraulein Westhoff had better be back on the project."

Assa replied with a slight smile, "That is good news, but you are still in no position to make demands."

Jacob followed up, "Fraulein Westhoff will be there. As I mentioned, I have a soft spot for you but do not force me to turn that into a hard object against you, like my brother would prefer. Auf Wiedersehen."

Titus was escorted out of the room, looked down the hallway where Westhoff was being kept, and tried to return back that way. The guard stopped him and led him in the other direction, out the front door of the villa. Titus was taken to the limousine and driven back to the Wall.

Back at the construction trailer area on the east side, he stepped out of the car, looked around in all directions. He was supposed to meet Herr Johann on the site but was ushered through the border checkpoint to the West. He walked away from the Wall on the west side and then turned back to it and addressed it as he would an adversary, "You have to go, somehow, some way."

Titus walked back to his hotel and noticed a light on in one of the construction trailers. He noticed it was the excavator's trailer, and he walked up the steps into the trailer. Upon entering, he did not see anyone inside, but he did hear some sounds in an enclosed area at the end of the trailer. Opening the door, he stepped in and looked around. It was a bare room with a simple mat on the floor. As he stepped in and onto the mat, the floor gave way, and Titus fell through the opening and landed on a pile of dirt. Next to him was a ladder leading up to the opening he had just fallen through.

He sat in the pile of dirt, thinking how his day was somehow getting worse, and now, feeling the impact of his fall, surprised he had not broken any bones. Waiting for his senses to settle, he looked up at the opening with the rug hanging down, then at the pile of dirt he was in, and then down the tunnel, which was a complete dirt-wall tunnel with lights in the distance. Titus pressed his hands down in the dirt, lifted himself up, and dusted himself off. *Now what? Something else trying to kill me?*

On his feet now, Titus looked in both directions of the tunnel and limped sorely in the direction toward the faraway lights in the tunnel. He could hear in the distance the sound of machinery. He crossed a tunnel that looked like an old brick sewer, full of loose dirt. What looked like aircraft bombs had been laid in a line in both directions down the sewer tunnel. Titus registered this as just another concern in his day so far.

He wiped the dirt off his pants and sleeves and continued past the brick sewer, deeper into the excavated tunnel, heading toward the lights. He approached a figure operating a small mechanical digger. The figure, who Titus could tell was a man in overalls, stopped the machine, sensing Titus's presence, and turned around with a Luger-style pistol in his hand. Titus recognized, in the dim light, that the man was the excavator Schlesinger.

Titus stepped back, raising his hands in front of him. "Hold on. It's just me, the architect."

The excavator lowered the pistol. "Aaach, so. Herr Dare, are you lost?" he asked with a slight grin.

"Probably. Are you trying to get ahead on the project or looking for buried treasure?" said Titus in a return jest, trying to defuse the confrontation.

"Bitte?" asked Schlesinger.

Titus thought about his wry comment and then remembered the map the excavator had been looking at in the trailer, "So that is what the map you had was for. You're trying to get to the underground bunker before it is unearthed by the building excavation, maybe before the twins do."

"Twins? Bunker? That is of no use to me. Leave that to the developer, as you call them, 'the twins.' From what I know, they like to play on both sides, but really only their own," said Schlesinger, attempting to return to his digging.

"So you do know them? I have had quite a visit with them today, at their villa."

Schlesinger paused, then, "Remember from the map, my father was in construction, too. The time before and after the war made a close circle of men, including the twins and my family. One had to, *has* to, keep one's friends and enemies close."

"Then what are you doing here, digging tunnels?" asked Titus, pointing towards the excavation.

The excavator looked at Titus closely. "I can trust you, I hope. I am trying to zimply get my family out. Your building is my opportunity. The excavation is my opportunity. If and when the building is rotated, I cannot get through to them on the East, so I need to do it now before the construction starts."

"So to where are you going tunneling, to the house of your family?" probed Titus.

"Alzo, the foundation-stone ceremony will allow certain East Germans close to the other side of the Wall," he continued. "That is my chance to get my family out. And your chances for a good life, Herr Dare, are not good down here. You must go back above and be the architect at the foundation-stone." He used the pistol as a pointer toward Titus and the way back out.

The excavator, still waving the pistol, started escorting Titus back the way he had entered the tunnel. Titus stopped and pointed at the brick sewer he had passed as they walked back, and then, with emphasis, he pointed at the bombs in the tunnel. "What is that tunnel? And are those what I think they are?"

"That is the tunnel, the false sewer under the street, under the Wall. You saw it on the old drawing I had."

"Right under the Wall? So that tunnel is indeed right under the Wall. Is that what the old drawing showed?" Titus asked, stopping for a moment.

"Ja, it was a very nice street at one time," remarked the excavator, pointing upward.

Looking up, Titus noted, "And that is a rather nasty crack developing in the tunnel masonry."

"Jawohl. The weight of the wall is right on the tunnel. One day, it will collapse, given the right push, but I cannot wait for that," said the excavator with a renewed sense of urgency in his voice.

"And your tunnel, your excavation, then, is heading to the east," said Titus, pointing down the tunnel.

"It is, unless I am a very bad excavator."

Titus started walking again. "Will you make it in time? How will you get them out? I can try to delay the foundation-stone ceremony somehow."

"That is why I am working now for tomorrow. I will come under the Baustellen Klo, how you say, porta potty on the east. And no, this is my . . . undertaking," smiling from his choice of words, "and nein, you should leave construction to the workers."

"And what the hell are those?" Titus asked, gesturing toward the line of bombs that lined the sewer.

"Those are gifts from your Air Force or maybe your British friends. They did not come to collect them after the war. I find them as I dig."

"Isn't that a little dangerous?"

"More dangerous than digging a tunnel into East Berlin? Besides, I am a good excavator, as I said."

"What if something goes wrong with your tunnel?"

"My relatives do not join me, but I will be joining them in the East, in prison."

"I think you are maybe crazy," Titus said. "Escape during a high-profile ceremony, tunneling under the Cold War, collecting bombs like souvenirs . . . and I thought I was living some dream, nightmare here, with only shabby cars trying to run me over."

"Aaach, crazy I am, maybe zo, but I am in good company," the excavator said, pausing with a point of his revolver at Titus. "But I could use your help. If you see something wrong up there at the ceremony, I need a, how you say, a distraction. That you could do."

"Trust me, they, the twins, the developer, will be watching me very closely. Not much I can do without being later dropped into a concrete foundation." Titus paused. "I wish I could get rid of the Wall," and turning to the excavator, "If I see anything, I will do something up there. I will leave you to it down here. Good luck, viel Glueck, and be careful with those," pointing to the bombs lying in the sewer.

Titus turned and headed back the way he came, climbing up the ladder and through the hole in the floor of the trailer. He placed the carpet back over the opening and exited the trailer. He glanced at the Wall as he exited the trailer, then walked away down the street and hailed a taxicab.

As the taxicab pulled up, Titus heard once again a familiar voice. "Hello again, my friend. We are making a good team," said the taxi driver, whom Titus now recognized as the driver from his past rides, thinking that the coincidence was probably just another aspect of Berlin's strange world.

"Good to see you, a friendly face after a long day," Titus said as he settled back in the seat but then leaned forward. "Are you a spy following me?"

"Ach, leider nicht, sorry no. Those jobs are all full here in Berlin, but we always need taxi drivers. I am not sure which is safer, taxi driver or spy."

Titus leaned back in the seat and tried to replay the last days in his head. Site visits, building problems, concrete burial, low-speed chase, gunfire, paradise, the police state, an offer that cannot be refused, unknown betrayal, bombs, and escape tunnels. *No, not like another day in the office.*

In the past he had interesting experiences when visiting the building sites of his projects and trying to resolve cultural differences, but this was at an extreme. His mental playback was interrupted by a jolt of the taxicab stopping in front of his hotel.

"My friend, it has been a pleasure, again," said the driver as he turned to Titus.

Titus fanned out his paper money for the man and remarked, "In case it is not an accident that we keep meeting, and to make it easy for you to find me, I will be leaving around 9:00 a.m. tomorrow."

The taxi driver pulled out a few bills and gave Titus a big smile. "I know already, but who does not?"

As the taxicab pulled away from the hotel, Titus noticed a

Trabant, with its lights in a haze of its own exhaust. *Perfect topper for the day. How could I have forgotten about you, my little smoke shadow?*

Titus walked past the desk clerk, who waved and offered, "Having a nice day with Berlin sightseeing?"

Titus answered, for his own benefit only, "Berlin is very intriguing, I will say," with a slight smile, then walked to the elevator door.

He entered his hotel room and looked all around, thinking how a hotel room of all things made him feel safe at this time . . . or maybe not. He proceeded to look in the bathroom and closets. Confirming he was alone, he sat down in the lounge chair and poured himself a drink from the bottle of water on the side table. He leaned his head back and closed his eyes, only to be disturbed from the peace by a knock on the door.

Titus rose from his chair and scooted over to the door, checking its lock before asking, "Who is it?"

"Potter," came the answer.

Titus opened the door with, "I am surprised you knocked. Third visitation so far. Are you the ghost of Berlin future?"

"Thought you could use a break from surprises," offered Potter as he stepped into the room with a nod of deference. "I understand you have made some progress on compromising despite your prima-donna architect nature. A change of heart, eh, Ebenezer?"

Potter moved to the room window and looked down at the street in both directions, then turned to face Titus.

Titus said, "Appreciate your thoughtfulness in knocking and insightful character assessment."

"Can you give me an update?" asked Potter.

"Frieda . . . Westhoff may have been a pawn in the change of my cooperation but maybe not with anything else. Either I do what the evil twins want, which is betting on the new Berlin and a DDR Disneyland, or it is curtains for me. Not an iron one but a concrete one."

"I see you have finally gained a sense of humor. Berlin is beginning to get into your veins, just have to keep your blood in them, and welcome to my world," Potter offered. "What about your buried bunker that you discovered?"

"Seems like a touchy subject, as that is when the threats started," replied Titus.

"I told you Hitler's secret hideaways made people here jumpy. But they let you go. They could have just jailed you for jaywalking or something. So, what is your plan now?"

"No idea. Go to the ceremony, say goodbye to Frieda . . . Westhoff, and go home, if I'm allowed. They're going to do what they want, and being a puppet for some East-West face-saving exercise is way beyond my design sensibilities, but it seems like architecture is not as important as politics. And why is it my plan? Aren't you spooks supposed to have all the countermeasures?"

Potter smiled. "Interesting assessment, and it sounds prudent about cooperating, but it's not like you to give in—or better put, to give up. It is your design and your integrity . . . and, unfortunately, your plan now. I will be working in the background."

Titus responded, "They have already made the decision to turn the building. I'm just a prop. They have Frieda as a prisoner and as bait for me. The twins will win no matter what side of the Wall they are on. I am only going back to the ceremony to see Frieda one more time. Maybe there is some way to get her out of this mess I got her into."

Potter thought for a moment. "Then best recommendation is to stay close to her at the ceremony, for any consolation in it for you. She is still a bargaining chip, it seems, in your mind as well as theirs, apparently. Maybe you can help her out, but any thought about using this little get-together at the Wall for an exit out of East Berlin for you two lovebirds is a bad idea. This current little détente surrounding your building is pretty fragile."

Titus focused on Potter. "Can't you get her out some way? Some spook move?"

"Wish I could help, but we already lost a part of one of our agents," said Potter.

"What do you mean by that? Is it Stecker? Is he alive?" asked Titus with surprise.

"Stecker showed up at our offices with a missing hand and wrist but still kicking. We're as surprised as you are. Apparently, he was at the factory, before you, and ran into some guards and then a stone-cutting machine. Would not let go of the listening bug he found in the concrete. Quite a resurrection, even for a spook," Potter said, "You still look like hell. Get some sleep. Busy day tomorrow."

Potter gave Titus a slight salute and headed to the door. Titus followed him and locked the door. He then looked around the room, threw his hands up, and fell backward onto the bed. He stared at the ceiling and thought about his choices. He could just depart Berlin, leave this nightmare behind, and be the architect he was. He could go through with the foundation-stone ceremony, see Frieda for a chance to say goodbye, and make sure this Berlin Tor never gets published as his opus. Or he could grab Frieda and a machine gun from a guard and shoot his way out.

He opened his eyes for a reality check. He was still in a hotel room in Berlin. Tomorrow was still tomorrow, and he had a decision to make but no choice.

Chapter Seven

Titus awoke the next morning, still in the clothes from last night. He sat up and looked at his face in the mirror over the dresser. He hardly recognized himself from when he first arrived in Berlin, then 'starchitect,' but now as a humbled pawn in a game. And a hostage. *Guess I should clean myself up for my execution*, was his consoling thought, and he headed to the bathroom for a shower.

After getting dressed, Titus headed out of his room and down to the hotel lobby. Exiting the hotel, he looked at the taxicab stand, and one of the taxicabs flashed its headlights at him. He waved to the taxicab, indicating he was going to walk to the Wall this time.

Titus arrived at the Wall, and the project site, paused for a deep breath, and walked to the checkpoint in the Wall. He entered, showed his documents, and headed to where the crowd had gathered around the foundation-stone on the east side. He made eye contact with the twins and then Westhoff, and as he tried to move closer to her, he was backed off by the surrounding guards. He had to restrain himself to a warm handshake with her, then repeat it with the other officials at the ceremony. He received a menacing look from the twins, followed by a weak handshake from each. Potter, standing among the group, gave him a reassuring look as the ceremony began with an official addressing the crowd.

Titus initially paid attention to the speech, but soon he

looked nervously around toward where the porta potty was, knowing it concealed the end point of the excavator's tunnel.

After an initial introduction, Jacob the twin was introduced, and he began, "Ladies and gentlemen, this is an important moment in Berlin, for this project reflects a new cooperation between the East and West. Hands of architecture reaching across a political division."

His twin brother Assa continued, "Meine Damen and Herrn, dies ist ein importantes Moment in Berlin, weil dieses Projeckt eine Kooperation zwischen Ost und West reflektiert. Haende von Architektur über eine politische Kluft hinweg."

Jacob said, "We are very . . . lucky to have the architect of our project on hand for this foundation-stone laying ceremony. He has been most accommodating in helping us make this project a bridge between German brothers."

Titus took this cue and started, "I see this as a portal, gateway . . . really."

As he looked at the twins, they each gave him a threatening stare, and the bodyguards standing behind Westhoff moved closer to her. Titus started to speak again but stopped when she looked at him with a warning expression. Titus stepped closer to her in an attempt to reassure her, but he remained silent now with a facial gesture of deference to the twins.

The ceremony continued with more speeches by the twins as they gathered around the foundation-stone. As they handed out the hammers for striking the stone, Titus noticed there was a disturbance in the crowd behind him. A guard came to the twins' side and whispered to one of them. The other guards started moving in the direction of the porta potty on the construction site, and because of the disturbance, Titus could move closer to Westhoff.

Titus could manage to whisper to Westhoff, "What is it?"

Westhoff whispered back, "Something about the toilet, how you say, porta potty, over there."

Titus now became nervous with the mention of the porta potty, realizing they may have found the end of the excavator's tunnel. He looked around for a way to bring the gathering's attention back to the ceremony. All he had for this was his voice, and he began shouting, "We have to turn the stone. It is facing the wrong direction. You have to turn it. The building has turned, so we have to turn it."

The twins looked at each other and back at Titus, who increased the agitation in his voice, repeating his demand as he eyed the guards heading to the porta potty. "The building is turned; we have to turn the stone," repeated Titus.

He continued shouting, addressing the gathered group, and gesturing with one of the hammers in his hand. The guards, who were heading to the porta potty, now noticed the disturbance caused by Titus. They turned, made eye contact with the twins, and started to head away from the direction of the porta potty and back to the ceremony area.

When the guards arrived, the twins gestured for Titus to be put on the other side of the Wall, on the west side. As there was some jostling around Titus by the guards, the ceremony group exchanged glances, some of concern and some of understanding. Titus looked toward Westhoff, but he was turned back by the guards, led away, and roughly escorted through the checkpoint to the West.

On the other side, Titus walked dejectedly away from the Wall, looking over his shoulder, and then started to run to the excavator's trailer, up the steps, and into the trailer. He went to the space where the concealed tunnel entry was and climbed down the ladder into the tunnel. He ran to the other end, where the excavator was already climbing up a ladder.

Titus shouted up to the excavator, "They, the East guards, know where the end of the tunnel is, just above you. You have to go back."

"Was? What about my Familie?" the excavator shouted in response, continuing up the ladder.

"You can get them out another way, another time," Titus said urgently looking up the ladder.

"Nein. Has to be now," affirmed the excavator.

"Are you sure they are up there in the crowd?"

"Ja. And they cannot go back," stated the excavator with a shake of his head.

Titus, looking around the tunnel, said, "There has to be a way of getting them out . . . and Frieda."

"Scheisse. Verdammte Mauer," said the excavator in total despair and frustration.

Titus looked back down the excavated tunnel and remembered the bombs on the sewer tunnel floor. "I have an idea. If they cannot get out under the Wall, then through the Wall. We'll blow it up, I mean, down."

"Was? Wie?" responded the excavator, with a glance at the tunnel opening above his head, seeming to lose hope.

"The sewer tunnel is right under the Wall. We'll blow open the top of the sewer and drop the Wall with the bombs. We just need something to set them off . . . without blowing us up."

"Warte mal. I have detonators for collapsing my tunnel after my family's escape if they came after us," said the excavator as he moved over to a metal box, grabbed a handful of detonators with a spool of detonation wire, and showed them to Titus.

"Better if you handle the detonators," said Titus, who grabbed the wire spool.

The excavator started to push detonators among the bombs lying in the dirt, and Titus started placing the wires along the top of the bombs.

As Titus returned from running the wire spool down the tunnel, the excavator said, "I will finish. Raus, get out of here. Go get Fraulein Westhoff away from the Wall. Give me a signal when she is safe. Here." He handed Titus a construction airhorn from a pile of excavation equipment.

Titus ran down the tunnel, climbed up the ladder, through the construction trailer, and jumped out the trailer door. He could not see what was happening on the other side of the Wall, but he noticed a wooden viewing stand for tourists nearby and ran to it for an overlook. He climbed up the platform and looked in the direction of the ceremony.

He could see the ceremony was continuing and made some direct but subdued gestures with his arms to attract the attention of Westhoff, who was standing in the group of ceremony officials. Luckily, Westhoff was also looking away from the group and to the West, and she finally saw him as he waved with more vigor from the viewing stand. He motioned for her to step away from the ceremony group.

Under the circumstances, this was a difficult thing to communicate without drawing attention to himself and to Westhoff.

She, however, could not at first grasp the warning, and he motioned to her again, more forcefully, with a backward wave of his hands.

She then backed out of the crowd slowly so as not to attract attention, but the guards now noticed Titus waving on the viewing stand across the Wall. They immediately started looking around for her in the crowd. Other guards were lifting the porta potty behind the ceremony. Looking back toward Westhoff, he saw that she was, once again, surrounded by the guards. He looked back to the porta potty, where the guards were looking under it into the tunnel.

There was no time to make a rational decision, no time to design an escape, only time to act against the Wall that separated him. Still standing on the platform, Titus looked toward where he had come out from underground at the excavator's trailer on his side of the Wall. Then he looked back to the East and could see the guards now entering the tunnel under the porta potty. He again looked for Westhoff and found her in the distance, still in the ceremony crowd surrounded by guards.

Feeling his fist clenching, he grasped the air horn in his hand, lifted it up, and gave a short blast. He could see Westhoff's eyes focus on him. He waved once again for her to move away, and then he started blowing the air horn continuously in the hope that Westhoff could break free as the attention of the crowd pivoted toward Titus.

In the group of eyes looking at him, he could make out those of one of the twins, who was motioning to an armed guard to take a shot at him. Titus hoped the shot would be above his head, that their aim was bad. At the sound of the shot, the crowd hunched downward, and Titus also ducked down on the viewing stand. The twin then motioned for the guard to pursue Titus through the checkpoint, and then both twins began gathering the attention of the group back to the ceremony to continue.

Titus stuck his head back up from the platform and watched to see where Westhoff was and if anyone was still paying attention to him. He could see the guards continuing to head down the tunnel on the other side of the Wall. The ceremony group was now crowded around the foundation-stone again as the twins were pressing the ceremony forward.

He started to blow the airhorn again as a continuous burst, just as one of the twins raised a hammer, the foundation-stone about to be tapped. As the hammer hit the stone, there was a loud explosion that knocked Titus to the deck of the platform.

The smoke and dust from the explosion engulfed the ceremony, and the dust cloud covered the whole area. Coughing and covering his mouth with his jacket, Titus raised himself up, but nothing was visible. As the wind blew the haze eastward, he peered over the Wall and saw that the length of the Wall in front of him had disappeared, dropped into a long slice of a trench in the ground, which still was billowing dust upward after the collapse.

Titus, with the construction horn still in his hand, assessed the situation as a surreal silence set in. Across the trench opening, he could see one of the twins with the ceremonial hammer in his hand, covered in dust. The surprise of the Wall's collapse was matched by the awkward stand-off of the situation, like a prisoner and law officer looking at each other through a not-very-good two-way mirror. The dust began to settle like dew on the ground, revealing more coughing, bewildered spectators.

He continued to stare across to the ceremony group, whose stare back at the missing Wall reflected the halo of disbelief as the quietness continued to surround the moment. The dust settled more, and the crowd stared across the opening in the ground in a surreal aura of time having stopped. Titus tried to focus on the faces of the twins, which were not registering any emotions, just dust-covered disbelief.

The shock of the Wall being gone began to slowly dissolve and register as an interesting opportunity. Suddenly, the crowd of spectators on the East began moving as a gentle wave to the West and where the Wall used to be.

Titus turned, started down the viewing platform, and ran toward the Wall, or at least where it had been. He stopped at the edge of the trench opening, and from this position, he tried to locate Westhoff through the faces of the dust-covered, stunned, but now-moving crowd.

He found a board plank to cross the trench, and once over the trench, his eyes searched for Westhoff, but he caught the twins' eyes instead, now focused on him. They were gesturing to the guards to shoot Titus. The guards pulled their guns to take aim, and Titus backed over the trench. In doing so, he caught sight of Westhoff struggling to get through the crowd. But the guards stopped her, and the despair on her face was unmistakable.

The shock, or trance, of the situation, ended with a sudden group shout and a rush of East Berliners running westward, sweeping through the ceremonial area.

This allowed Westhoff to back up, away from the group of guards and amidst the onrushing East Berliners, who had started placing planks and construction rails over the trench. They ran past Titus to the West. A Trabant, honking and full of East Germans, drove over the trench of the Wall on the makeshift planks and scaffolding rails. It passed close to him, with the driver focused straight ahead to the West and the passengers waving at Titus. Despite the hazardous circumstance, he could only smile that the car was not trying to run him over.

As Westhoff started to be pushed with the crowd to the West, the guards caught sight of her movement and started shooting into the air to clear the crowd around them so they could grab her. Other guards and now soldiers were moving to the wall trench to stop the people from crossing over from East to West.

A second wave of East Berliners, larger than the first wave, overwhelmed the group of guards and soldiers trying to stop the crowd. This allowed Westhoff to break free, and she looked up at the building crane on the east side of the Wall. The boom arm was high above over the top of the trench, and the crane cable was hanging down to the west side. She headed to the base of a tower crane and started climbing up the ladders of the crane's shaft, heading toward the operator's cabin.

Watching her, Titus noticed the similar tower crane on the west side and started heading to its base. He also started to climb up the ladders of the crane shaft on his side of the Wall.

As Titus climbed up, he looked down at the confusion on both sides of the Wall. East Berliners were rushing across the trench, and West Berliners were helping them across the trench, absorbing them into the crowd. The soldiers, now completely overwhelmed, were still trying to secure what was the former barrier of the Wall.

The realization of the absurdity of the situation, of how his current climb was going to possibly reunite him with Westhoff, was heightened by Titus's sense of how high he had climbed. He could now see that the guards from the ceremony were climbing after Westhoff, as well as watching Titus's ascent.

While climbing up the crane may have seemed an escape from the guards at the ceremony, Westhoff was now faced with a possible dead-end route. The only path for her escape would be climbing out on the horizontal jib to the trolley and hook that was currently positioned close to the west side of the Wall.

As she looked out over the jib, she could see that Titus had reached the cabin of the tower crane on the west side. He was waving to get her attention and also looking at the crane controls to move his crane jib toward hers. Panic can create a certain clarity, and he was able to start up the crane engine and then took his best guess at how to rotate the crane.

Westhoff looked at her crane controls at the same time and also started her crane engine. Her jib had only a short distance to go to meet Titus's crane, but the crane stopped rotating as she moved it. She tried again and could hear the clang of some metal control regulator as the rotation stopped. Looking down to see what the blockage was, she noticed the guards were now halfway up the crane ladder toward the cabin. She tried again to rotate the crane, hoping to break through whatever it was that had stopped the crane.

The twins, still standing by the foundation-stone and engulfed by more of the East Berliners heading to the West, noticed the clanging sound above the noise of the crowd. Looking up, they saw Westhoff in the crane control cabin above, with the guards ascending the ladder from the base. At the same time, they also noticed the movement of Titus's crane on the west side and could see Titus in the control cabin of that crane.

Titus managed to turn his crane jib over the top of the Wall without any rotation block and to almost touch Westhoff's jib, but his was slightly below hers. He waved her forward to climb out across the horizontal jib on her crane toward the jib on his crane. As he started to climb out of the control cabin, a single shot rang out from below, directed at Westhoff as a warning.

Westhoff looked at Titus for encouragement, and then she started moving out along the jib. Titus continued to climb out along his crane to reach hers. More gunshots rang out, ricocheting off of the steel framework, and Westhoff stopped moving forward. Titus, however, pushed onward and reached the end of his crane.

Looking up at Westhoff and then beyond to the guards, who were now at the control cabin, Titus had a difficult choice but no options. He looked up again and tried to grab the cable hook hanging down from her crane. He could see that Westhoff had started climbing back out to meet him again. Her only chance now was to reach the end of her crane and climb down the cable to where Titus was on his crane jib.

Hesitating at the climb down a cable, Westhoff looked back over her shoulder to see that a soldier was seated at the controls of her crane. She reached down for the cable and could feel the crane frame begin to vibrate underneath her.

The crane boom started to move, and Westhoff, to the surprise of Titus, pulled a gun out of her pants, the one he had seen in her briefcase, he presumed. She aimed and fired a shot at the guard at the controls in the cabin. She then reached down for the cable again, dropping the pistol and grabbing the cable with both hands, but before she could swing her feet down to grasp the cable, the crane began to rotate. Westhoff froze as the cable began to swing.

"Jump, you have to jump, now!" yelled Titus.

The guards below had temporarily stopped shooting but began again, firing single shots at both Titus and Westhoff. Looking back along the crane and then down to Titus, she had no choice but to jump toward Titus, who managed to hold on to her from his own precarious position. He pulled her up onto his crane jib. As they climbed back along the framework, the clang of bullets striking the metal structure continued but then suddenly stopped.

Titus looked back over his shoulder, with his arm around Westhoff, and could see that the crowd below had finally pushed through the line of guards that had arrived on the east side of the construction site. The crowd had swarmed past the guards and soldiers, and the push of the crowd was now like a huge wave washing up on the shoreline of where the Wall used to be.

Titus and Westhoff continued along the horizontal jib to the vertical part of the crane where the control cabin was, then started to climb down the crane ladder. When they reached the base of the crane and were on the ground, groups of East Berliners and West Berliners were swirling around, uniting and rejoicing.

The crowd kept pushing west and pulled Titus and Westhoff along until Titus could grab the door handle of a car, a Trabant, that had been abandoned after its inhabitants had reached the West. He pulled himself up on the hood of the car and then hoisted Westhoff up as well. Together, they climbed to the roof of the car for a better view of the spectacle.

Looking around the scene to the west, Titus caught sight of the excavator climbing out of his construction trailer, darkened with smoke and dirt but grinning as his relatives from the East surrounded him. Embracing Westhoff, Titus waved to the excavator, who beamed a smile back to Titus with his hands clasped over his head in victory.

And then looking eastward, Titus could see Potter standing on the foundation-stone with a large smile as the crowds continued past the twins, who were still standing by the foundation-stone but who had been swallowed by the push of the escape to the West.

Titus and Westhoff climbed down from the car's roof and started walking westward with the crowd that started to disperse down the streets of West Berlin. In the thinning crowds, there stood a single

West Berlin taxicab, with Titus's friendly driver standing there, wearing a broad grin. He greeted them with, "I see West has met East, a reunification, I think it is called. Na, wohin? Where to?"

Titus gave Westhoff a large kiss in an embrace, and they climbed into the taxicab and drove off to the West.

The End

About The Author

Paul Krieger is an architect in Chicago who studied and worked in West Berlin in 1982. While the Berlin Wall was an unfriendly presence in Berlin, he was interested in its relentless architectural impact on the divided city. His wedding anniversary is on the date of the erecting of the Berlin Wall.

www.ingramcontent.com/pod-product-compliance
Lightning Source LLC
Chambersburg PA
CBHW060450310726

48977CB00001B/389